SPHINX

Introduction by
Daniel Levin Becker

ANNE GARRÉTA

TRANSLATED FROM THE FRENCH BY
EMMA RAMADAN

The first genderless novel ever writt[e]
linguistic and literary accomplishn[ent]
intricacies of Monique Wittig and Roland Barthes with the ornate language of Alan Hollinghurst. Garréta's debut novel at twenty-three years old, *Sphinx* was published in France in 1986 to universal acclaim and gained the author admittance into the prestigious Oulipo literary collective in 2000. *Sphinx* is a modern classic of experimental, feminist, and queer literature, translated into five languages but never before published in English. This publication marks the first full-length work by a female member of the Oulipo to ever be published in English.

. . . .

More praise for Sphinx*:*

"...a bold, strange, perfectly constructed novel." —EVA DOMENEGHINI

"A literary feat...The most beautiful praise one can give to a novel is to say that it is unlike anything else...What she has done is a kind of masterpiece." —JACQUES LAURENT

"Astonishing." —SYLVIE GENEVOIX, *Madame Figaro*

"One wonders whether Anne Garréta, who thinks of everything, thought of the nightmare she was setting up for her translators—into English, for example, where the possessive, *his, her,* agrees with the subject?" —MICHELLE BERNSTEIN, *Chronique*

"A remarkable entrance into the literary scene... A first novel so promising that it foreshadows, one hopes, a long literary career." —JOYSANE SAVIGNEAU, *Le Monde*

"Anne Garréta has achieved what is certainly the most difficult and rarest feat in a first novel-memoire: she disconcerts the reader." —ANDRÉ BRINCOURT, *Le Figaro*

SPHINX

SPHINX

—

Anne Garréta

TRANSLATED FROM THE FRENCH BY
EMMA RAMADAN

INTRODUCTION BY
DANIEL LEVIN BECKER

DEEP VELLUM PUBLISHING
DALLAS, TEXAS

Deep Vellum Publishing

2919 Commerce St. #159, Dallas, Texas 75226

deepvellum.org · @deepvellum

ISBN: 978-1-941920-09-1 (paperback) · 978-1-941920-08-4 (ebook)

LIBRARY OF CONGRESS CONTROL NUMBER: 2015930301

—

*Cet ouvrage, publié dans le cadre d'un programme d'aide à la publication,
bénéficie du soutien du Ministère des Affaires étrangères et du
Service Culturel de l'Ambassade de France aux Etats-Unis.*

This work, published as part of a program of aid for publication,
received support from the French Ministry of Foreign Affairs and the
Cultural Services of the French Embassy in the United States.

—

Cover design & typesetting by Anna Zylicz · annazylicz.com

Text set in Bembo, a typeface modeled on typefaces cut by Francesco Griffo
for Aldo Manuzio's printing of *De Aetna* in 1495 in Venice.

Deep Vellum titles are published under the fiscal sponsorship of
The Writer's Garret, a nationally recognized nonprofit literary arts organization.

Distributed by Consortium Book Sales & Distribution.

Printed in the United States of America on acid-free paper.

To the third

INTRODUCTION

An anecdote that may be instructive to the reader of novels written under Oulipian constraint: in 1969, after Georges Perec published *La Disparition*—if not the most illustrative example of an Oulipian novel then certainly the easiest to explain[1]—a critic named René-Marill Albérès reviewed it, lukewarmly, in the journal *Les Nouvelles littéraires*. Other critics reviewed *La Disparition* too, of course; what stood out about Albérès was that he plainly missed the central conceit of the book, namely that it had been written without any words containing the letter E.

I bring this up because, whatever grim conclusions we may reach specific to Albérès's deftness as a reader (and *La Disparition* takes place in a world from which the letter E has gone mysteriously missing, so it's not like there weren't clues), his gaffe points out a pitfall with the potential to trip up even the most meticulous littérateur: reading an Oulipian novel without knowing the precise way in which it is Oulipian.

Did I say pitfall? I might have meant windfall.

As types of vertigo go, after all, being in the Oulipian dark is not such a bad one. It can even be refreshing, given that most novels in this milieu are preceded at some distance by their reputations. But in any

---

1   Speaking of explanations, the adjective Oulipian is retrofitted from the name OuLiPo, which stands for ouvroir de littérature potentielle, or workshop for potential literature: a collective established in Paris in 1960 with the purpose of exploring and exploiting the generative literary potential of linguistic, mathematical, and scientific structures—which, lots of the time, is a fancy way of saying the use of constraints as a writing aid. Perec became a member of the Oulipo in 1967 (and is still a member despite having died in 1982, according to one of the group's admittedly stringent bylaws). Anne Garréta, on whom more in a moment, became a member in 2000, and I became one in 2009.

case let's continue to treat the situation with gravity, so to speak, for a moment longer.

The first time I read *Sphinx*, Anne Garréta's first novel, I knew that it was Oulipian,[2] but not how. It took me about forty pages to figure out its conceit, and what I felt once I did was more than just relief, more than just satisfaction to have quieted that nagging sense of missing something: I was, well, still bewildered. But it was a refreshing, trees-to-forest kind of bewilderment, the kind that comes when, say, you've been so busy trying to put together a jigsaw puzzle that you're caught off guard by how strange and fascinating the resulting picture is. A bewilderment that asks not *what* but *how*. Like its namesake from Greek myth, *Sphinx* was that rare riddle that only makes you think harder after you know the answer.

Now, I assume that if you're here you already know the answer, such as it is: you know the unspoken constraint behind the novel you are about to read, or have maybe just finished. (If you happen *not* to know the answer yet, I urge you to do everything in your power to stay ignorant for a while longer: sheathe the front and back covers of the book in kraft paper, avoid discussing it with booksellers, and don't read any reviews unless you're confident that they were written by lousy, inattentive critics. One hint: Anne Garréta uses the letter E plenty of times herein—your quarry lies elsewhere.)

Here's the thing about *Sphinx*, though: it will bewilder you no matter which side of the riddle you enter from. The reader who knows what he or she is getting into from the outset loses nothing of the novel's

---

2   This is actually a much more complex and debatable statement than it seems. First of all, there is a longstanding debate within and without the Oulipo as to whether any work should be called Oulipian simply because its author is a member of the Oulipo. (Is this introduction Oulipian?) Second of all, even if you respond yes to the first point, there is still the technicality that Garréta published *Sphinx* in 1986, fourteen years before she became an Oulipian. In any event, at the time of my first reading the book had been commended to me as Oulipian by a trusted source, and I do not feel I was led astray.

true vertigo—the high-wire act by which Garréta, under the cover of a relatively conventional narrative, quietly dismantles various conventions in the way we think and speak about love and despair and need. It bewilders me still, less on the technical level than on the level at which the technical merges with the conceptual, the medium with the message. To read *Sphinx* already aware of its conceit is only to break the picture back into its constituent puzzle pieces, to reverse the sequence of the questions your bewilderment asks: to go in wondering how the novelist pulled off this one trick,[3] but come out wondering what kind of reality you've been inhabiting.

Above and beyond constraint, that particular blend of readerly effort and figure-ground reversal is one of the best things an Oulipian novel can hope to achieve, and in that sense *Sphinx* is consummately Oulipian. It's worth noting, I suppose, that in other senses it is not remotely: stylistically, for one thing, it has none of the lightness, none of the gleeful air of structured play, found in most Oulipian fiction. Garréta's prose is heavy, drastic, baroque, at once ruthlessly clinical and deeply sentimental; her characters wage their struggles against language and its strictures not out of a desire to explore or make mischief, but based on stakes of life and death. Sometimes literally, depending on the book.[4]

Nonetheless, even if Garréta is an unusually ornate stylist for the Oulipo, and arguably the most deliberately radical thinker it has ever

---

3   To say nothing of the translator. If Garréta's composition of *Sphinx* was a high-wire act, then Emma Ramadan's task in carrying it over into a language with at least one crucially important constitutional difference is, near as I can figure it, akin to one tightrope walker mimicking the high-wire act of a second walker on a steeply diverging tightrope, while also doing a handstand.

4   The two other novels Garréta published prior to joining the Oulipo, *Ciels liquides* (1990) and *La Décomposition* (1999), are excellent examples of the class of modern French novel or film that sounds charming and fun when you hear its synopsis but turns out to be sort of existentially upsetting when you actually read or watch it.

counted among its ranks, she still belongs in those ranks, and *Sphinx* shows why. Like the best of the workshop's productions, it is animated by a drive to use language to question language, to manipulate and master and subvert the mechanics of everyday expression. In doing so it creates a subtly but sometimes chillingly different world, one that arises not so much within the narrative as within our experience of reading it. And it leaves us to sort out the implications, mostly, once we learn to recognize them: the arbitrariness of our assumptions; the flimsiness of our institutions; the difficulties of knowing another person, oneself, anything. Pitfall, windfall. The vertigo changes but does not disappear.

Daniel Levin Becker
San Francisco, January 2015

I

Remembering saddens me still, even years later. How many exactly, I don't know anymore. Ten or maybe thirteen. And why do I always live only in memory? Soul heavy from too much knowing, body tired from feeling pensive and powerless at the same time, so riven by this obsessive ennui that nothing, or almost nothing, can distract it anymore. Back then, if I recall correctly, I used to describe the world as a theater where processions of corpses danced in a macabre ball of drives and desires. My contempt and ennui did not, however, keep me from observing how this dance dissolved into an amorous waltz. Languid nights at the whim of syncopated rhythms and fleeting pulses; the road to hell was lit with pale lanterns; the bottom of the abyss drew closer indefinitely; I moved through the smooth insides of a whirlwind and gazed at deformed images of ecstatic bodies in the slow, hoarse death rattle of tortured flesh.

But I was slipping and could only keep falling; I couldn't cut myself off or break from my destiny with a mesmerized flight. Is it blasphemy to insist that my lucid crossing to hell was a direct road to redemption? "You would not look for me if you had not found me; you would not long for me if you had not once held me in your arms."

Those arms, the intense sweetness, a series of scenes that still ignites a carnal flame in my memory. A★★★ was a dancer. I would spend my nights waiting for A★★★ to appear on the stage of the Eden, a cabaret on the Left Bank. And who wouldn't have been enamored of that svelte frame, that musculature seemingly sculpted by Michelangelo, that satiny skin far superior to anything I had ever known?

In those years I was the resident DJ at the Apocryphe, a fashionable nightclub at the time.

* * * * * * * * * * * * * *

I've been trying unsuccessfully to remember the first visions I had of A★★★. Without a calling, I drift through the world with no control over my explosions of delirious happiness or my collapses into despair. I am easily distracted, ready for the most random deviations. So I must have first spotted A★★★ during a melancholic, disinterested contemplation of a succession of bodies I wasn't trying hard to distinguish, on the stage of a cabaret where some obliging alcoholic had decided to drag me, coming from a club where we'd mingled our disappointments. Asking myself afterward what had made the place so appealing, I couldn't describe it. In that blur, something must have struck me: something started operating underground, a digging, a tunneling in my mind following the blinding impact of a fragment on my retina. A body, just one, that I hadn't identified, surreptitiously had filled the place with a seduction that permeated so deeply I couldn't discover the cause, I couldn't uncover the root of it.

* * * * * * * * * * * * * *

Not long after that first outing at the Eden, Tiff, one of my friends of the time who had recently become an exotic dancer after her stint as an acrobat, dragged me along on her usual tour of cabarets. I was finally being granted what I had been after for a long time: the chance to be the shadow of a body whose own is stolen by the spotlight. She had agreed to meet me around ten one night, in one of the big cafés on the Place Pigalle. It was autumn. On my way there, I was walking against the current in a flood of hurried men, watchful men with a careful step— where were they going to in such a rush? A streetwalker crossed my path, harnessed in garters and leather straps. Her joints, limbs, and torso were bound in black leather fastened with metallic buckles. On the edge of the sidewalk she began her firefly ballet. She looked like a gladiator, or some kind of beast of burden. All along the boulevard these stores—half sex shop, half erotic lingerie shop—offered the elements of such ensembles. A little farther along, I stopped in front of one of the half-curtained storefronts. Were there really women who wore these blood-red bodices, purple garter belts, and sheer lace thongs? I was continuing on my way when, passing through the halo of light projected onto the pavement from the entrance of a cabaret, I suddenly recalled the spotlight cast on that body dancing the finale on the stage of the Eden. The desire to go back pulsed through me—the fleeting feeling that I had left something behind there.

I sped up until I reached the café on the northwest corner of the Place Pigalle. Some working-class men in tired suits were packed tightly together along the bar. The neon dripped a muggy light on this anxious sampling of humanity. Tiff was standing near the cash register talking to one of the servers. I recognized her thanks to the shimmer of her rhinestones and sequins shining dimly through a thick cloud of cigarette smoke. Tiff would always start yelling out to me as soon as she saw me. Her shortsightedness, which she refused to correct out of vanity, thankfully limited the range of her shouts—a hello accompanied by so many affectionate names that it had made me blush at the beginning of our friendship. In this café filled with the lingering stench of anxiety and brutality, hearing myself called "my love" and "my pet" sent shivers of nervousness and dread down my spine. In the clash of Arabic sounds and the servers' shouts, I thought such an outburst would make the world stop spinning. But no one seemed to have noticed—to have heard—what was worrying me so much. It was as if I was acting as a sound box, involuntarily amplifying all the words and noises swirling around me. It was painful listening to the inane music of the pinball machine, the sound of people banging on it, as if each strike were a blow against my skull. In a flash of magnesium, Tiff's voice bore into my brain. A distant shock continued to spread inside of me, the tremors inciting fear of a potential fragility. A pang at the thought of the Eden, still haunting me, led to the first rip: a tear in the veil that was suffocating my thoughts, completely laying them bare to the surrounding sharpness.

She ordered us both a brandy and a coffee and announced our nocturnal itinerary: a dozen cabarets from Pigalle to Opéra, dives and spectacles of fake luxury where the same strippers strutted every fifteen minutes, turning tirelessly from stage to stage. She was describing hell to me with the frivolity of the damned. Due to the combined effect of a very hot coffee and a very dry cognac, I felt a sharp burn in my throat; the perfumed haze radiating down my sinuses blurred my eyes with tears. She noticed: "My child, when you are barely weaned from your mother's milk, don't go venturing into places this cheap to drink liquor this strong." "My love," "my child"—we made each other burst out laughing.

This tour of cabarets was only a pretext to pursue a major passion of mine: the contemplation of bodies. Passion—arbitrary, blind, and indifferent—needs only to feed off of its own intensity to achieve the paroxysm of its pleasure: its object is of no consequence, chosen arbitrarily and without discrimination. I did the rounds of the professional ballets and the cabarets without distinguishing between the two; the prima ballerina was worth the same to me as the stripper. What could pass for vice or for bad taste was merely the result of a haughty ignorance of relative values. Beauty is just as vapid as its distinctions. I was running after the sublime, where everything is good. I was chasing after an image of ruffled sails that raise themselves like a phantom ship on a sea of oil, drifting, coming together, breaking free at the command of imperceptible trade winds, trailing around an infinite sorrow to the four corners of the stage. And whether the ship was a galley, a schooner, a merchant ship, or a privateer vessel didn't matter. What did I care whether it put up its sails or slowly stripped itself bare? Its wandering was what moved me. I spent the night drifting from port to port. While waiting for Tiff, I wallowed in seedy dressing rooms which were in reality mere landings between two flights of stairs, blocked off with battered chairs and cardboard boxes surrounded by bottles of fizzled-out sparkling wine under the gray of a flaking ceiling. I observed the hellish comings and goings of strippers dashing around, dressing, undressing, touching up their makeup, fixing their outfits, and spraying perfume; I gazed at myself distractedly in a mirror imprinted with lipstick and etched with clumsy letters. The wheezing of the ceiling fan, the rumble from the nearby stage, the sight of the red velvet sofa covered in holes, burned through by cigarettes, and the feeling of exile between blue walls defiled with the imprints of dirty hands brought me all the closer to that single, splenetic feeling so difficult to define: melancholia. I relished it to the point of drunkenness. In this refuge, a haven of ennui, I could give myself up freely to a vision of bodies shiny with sweat, stranded and exposed under the blind eye of the spotlight, infected by the dampness and stuffy stench of a mob crouching in the shadows of the stage. And here I found what I had come looking for: before my eyes, a sweltering, vitrified clash of light and flesh in the swaying red darkness.

The Black-Jack and the Tahiti had closed two days before after a raid by the vice squad. That left us around forty-five minutes of free time. Our next stop was at the Ambigu, one of the last remaining cabarets of the golden age of Montparnasse. We crossed over the Seine by Pont Neuf. Tiff drove too fast for me to enjoy the ride; I was in the grips of an excited trembling from this race through the almost-empty streets of Paris—from the speed, the solemn desertedness of the city, the violent contrast between the lights and their shadows.

A small roadblock in a little street perpendicular to the banks forced us to slow down, and I recognized the entrance to the Eden, still lit up, as we passed. Tiff, noticing my lingering gaze, suggested we go in to have a drink and see some friends. I was in such a rush getting out of the car that she had a hard time keeping up with me in her high heels. Once inside, we said some hurried hellos to the host, the cashier, and the coat checker, and then Tiff led me toward the wings of the stage. The neon dazzled me right away. In front of the mirrors was a row of half-naked women taking off their makeup. I barely had time to observe them before Tiff was dragging me along with her through a maze of doors and stairs toward the dressing rooms of the lead dancers. At the end of the corridor we crossed paths with someone I would come to know later as A★★★, who, head shaved, was now coming out of the dressing room to perform the finale: the descent down a big staircase lined with a teeming wall of black and white feathers. The show was drawing to a close. The dressing rooms were abuzz with assistants gathering costumes and dancers hurriedly removing their makeup. Tiff introduced me to one of the leads, also one of her old acrobatic partners. Strangely enough, some of these people recognized me from the Apocryphe or some other club where they would go dancing for their own enjoyment once the show was over.

We had just enough time to exchange a number of hellos and to have a drink before leaving again for the eighth cabaret of the night. The visit to the Eden was a brief respite in this race that made up a typical night for Tiff. I had been in so many cabarets that they all started to look the same by five in the morning: a sweaty inferno, a bombardment of lighting alternatively seedy and brash, a night striped with so many lights that there was neither dusk nor dawn.

By the end of her treks, Tiff always found herself with feet bruised from high-heeled shoes and back aching from lugging her bags of stage costumes from her car to her dismal dressing rooms. Always in a rush, Tiff would grab the reward for her performance on the way out (between twenty and sixty francs depending on the quality of the establishment). She dropped me off at my door. As I leaned in to say goodnight, her perfume caught my attention. What was it called again, and what did it remind me of? The question nagged at me for a long time before I managed to fall asleep. The next evening, on the way home from buying vinyl records for the Apocryphe, I passed in front of the Guerlain boutique on the Champs-Elysées and the name abruptly came back to me: Parure.

The Eden held a certain power over me; I was helpless against it. Before I went to work at night, I would spend two hours there, from ten to midnight. The troupe very quickly adopted me: they asked for my opinion on their makeup and confessed to me all their little dramas. I liked to let myself be brushed by naked skin, by boas and feather fans. I liked to watch as a face transformed under the stroke of a pencil and the touch of a brush, the line of a drawn eyebrow, the shape of an accentuated cheekbone. This living exhibition turned me off of antiquities; the odors of perfume and sweat were missing at all the museums I visited.

Out of all the dancers, A★★★ showed the most enthusiastic fondness toward me. Our relationship was very ceremonious at first. I would follow A★★★ into the dressing room, often bringing along a token of my affection: flowers; a photograph taken surreptitiously as A★★★ entered onto the stage; a fashion etching from the 1930s. My attempt at courtship was like something out of a book from the 19th century.

After the kiss on the lips that everyone there was rewarded with upon arrival, I would listen to the details of A★★★'s day. I would settle deep into the red velvet couch in the dressing room, stretching my legs over the armrest, and silently contemplate the slow process of applying makeup and arranging a costume. I noticed ironically that the dancers spent more time adjusting these little delicate nothings that elude nudity than one would dressing oneself from head to toe for a gala at the Opéra.

There are a thousand details to consider when putting on a simple g-string that never even cross the mind of the socialite pulling on her long gown or the man fastening a bow tie on the wing collar of his shirt. A thousand details in order to show off a behind, leaving the thighs and hips free and visible, but without revealing the crotch. I was amazed at the time it took for a body always to appear smooth, hairless, supple, and flawless: in a word, angelic. I learned that black skin like A★★★'s demands makeup of a completely different hue and variety than white skin. I learned how fragile the body is, how much care is required to maintain the suppleness of the limbs and joints. Before leaving the dressing room, A★★★ always performed a few dance steps for my selfish pleasure; then we would separate. The last image I had before going to work was of the shimmering golden reflections on skin lit up by dim hallways lights and soon devoured by the shadows of the wings. I would linger for a few moments in the dressing room, contemplating all the tools of meta-morphosis, the street clothes lying around. Often I would dreamily put back an object that had fallen on the floor, or leave a little note slipped between the mirror and its frame. It wasn't the show that brought me to the Eden; I would hurry toward the exit while the audience applauded the opening, sitting with their champagne. Once outside, I would make my way on foot to the Apocryphe, progressively sobering up over the fifteen-minute walk that I always took, regardless of the weather or the season.

· · · · · · · · · · · · · · ·

The Apocryphe! Dark nights light up with red. Somewhere between brothel and butcher shop, its ambiguous essence was never revealed except to those who knew how to decipher mirrors' reflections. One had to guess at everything, trying to grasp words on lips, fugitive gestures, events captured in the mirror, while pretending to stare at oneself. A macabre masked ball, people tripping over streamers that snaked down from the ceiling and coiled around the supporting pillars. To distill music, to set bodies in rhythm, was to be the priest of a harrowing cult. Once I realized that, all I could do was drift, asking myself why I was there, besides the chance that had brought me and the poisonous ease that had ensnared me. Then again, why leave? It was so easy to think of this crossing over as a trial of purification through the mud. I would have had to pretend to look all over again for some kind of calling, knowing full well that there was nothing to find, and that it would all end in horror and silence.

The moment I started there coincided with my decision to abandon what could have been an honest intellectual career. I had wasted four or five years on the benches of my school's theology department. Had I really imagined entering into a religious practice? I was about to launch into a thesis when, for some strange reason, a profound refusal began to bubble up in me. Not a refusal of faith or of metaphysics, but of the inanity of the scholarly discourse the university required me to use. The incomprehension of my fellow students, their constant tendency to relate every idea to some troubling personal decision and thus to consider the slightest original thought as the expression of an individual vice, only added to my melancholy and disgust. I was put on trial for everything I said, and so I adopted a seemingly contemptuous silence. I deserted my courses and avoided the cafés where the new inquisitors gathered and instead took refuge at my house, reading the books left behind long ago in the apartment my grandmother had bequeathed to me. For six months, from October to March, I succumbed to my natural tendency for reclusion, living between my bed and my desk.

I avoided going to the university as much as possible; the idea horrified me. But I went to the lectures on the Incarnation given on certain Thursdays by Padre★★★, a Spanish Jesuit. One day as I was leaving his class, he called me over, suggesting we have dinner together. The invitation was so casual, even bordering on nonchalant, that it seemed only natural to accept. Padre★★★ practiced his faith in the strictest orthodoxy, though some people accused him of violating its core commandments in his private life. Apparently he didn't flee from worldly activities with sufficient horror. Because he wrote a column on culture for one of the larger evening newspapers and was the cofounder of a gastronomic circle, the students considered him a scandalous hypocrite, a deviant of decadent habits, which, I confess, made him pretty interesting to me. And so without hesitating I accepted his invitation for the next day.

Over dinner we vaguely alluded to the path it seemed I was about to quit. I think he understood my reasons for defecting and approved of them, but didn't want to admit it. When I entered into the world of theology, I had aroused hope in many of the priests and professors, due as much to my own intellectual merit as to the overall intellectual weakness of the sons and daughters of well-established families who had devoted themselves to these studies. I inexplicably wasn't living up to their hope that if I didn't take the vow I would at least become a respectable doctor in theology who might bring back a bit of luster to the discipline, devalued as it was by the mediocrity of its traditional followers; the Church pines for these lights of Reason as much as it fears them. Young Catholics born, raised, and nurtured in the accepted family faith tend to lack audacity. Restricted by tight-laced morals, they retreat from thought as soon as a question comes beating too furiously against the flanks of their fortified certitudes. Doomed to inbreeding according to hallowed rituals, they shrink from all secular currents that aren't weighed down by dogmas. The young girls, sensible and stupid, reserving their virginity for their husbands; the young men of old France, equally timid and crude under the contradictory effect of a suppressed sensuality that finds its outlet in military endeavors or during religious charity trips.

Most of the participants of these theological cycles replaced intelligence and pertinence with narrow-minded diligence and a stubborn naïveté that nothing could disarm. The result was a sanctimonious flock that couldn't countenance the idea that the purpose of philosophy was not to posit an unequivocal certitude, crying out body and soul to designate the "good" philosophy and condemn in turn the "bad." They all congregated in the class of a theologian from Freiburg who specialized in this type of anathema. He stoked their base passions and exorcised their terrors. I attended his first class. He was determined to separate the proper from the improper in the ideas of our era. In the space of an hour, he derided all that had left its mark on the culture over the past two centuries. The audience was delighted at having within their grasp the arguments of someone in a position of authority, which had hitherto been cruelly lacking in their struggle against the materialists, dialecticians, analysts, and other genealogists. I never set foot in his class again after a heated discussion in which he placed all of his opponents—myself among them—at the mercy of his devout followers. They formed a cabal: they spoke of killing the black sheep; of the Freemasonry of relapsed Jews; of communists bankrolled by speculative German thought; of libidinal intellectuals conceived on the divans of cosmopolitanism. The lack of decorum in the debate, as much his archaic behavior, distressed me immeasurably. In the face of this crowd of imbeciles that prided itself on the title of "the Lord's flock," I was deciding whether to resort to violence or haughty resignation. I prayed ironically for this flock to transform into a blazing spit roast, or at least for the arrival of a blistering epidemic of brucellosis, neither of which ever came about.

This bad quarrel rendered the studious path odious to me and was the final push in my decision to stray from it. I took up the habit of studying in complete solitude at my house, and I would show up to the university exams without having attended any of the lectures. Padre★★★ directed my thesis, which I wrote in part while in residence at Solesmes Abbey for three weeks of perfect tranquility, benefiting from the resources of the Benedictine library.

One night we dined well in one of the Padre's favorite restaurants. Over liqueur, after we had finished discussing the thousand problems we faced at the university, he proposed an outing he thought I might like, to a very exclusive nightclub where he was a member. The idea that a priest, in his cassock no less, could frequent these places that the traditional bourgeoisie condemn as places of debauchery might scandalize naïve souls. But in such places I encountered so many people that one would never expect to find there, and witnessed so many scenes that one would think implausible, that the slight surprise I felt then seems to me, retrospectively, to be the mark of an almost ridiculous simplicity. I didn't take the Padre for a saint, I didn't think it improper that a priest went to these places of pleasure, nor even that he went there habitually, and I was no doubt guilty of still more shameful slumming. But the contrast between our pious conversation in the calm of a private room and the surging of music and movement that we would certainly encounter in this club shocked me prophetically, so to speak.

We had to take a taxi there. It was raining, one of those April showers that unfolded a moving curtain of icy pleats in the troubled night air. We sat in silence. I don't know what the Padre was thinking about but I suspect he was observing me, looking straight ahead of him at the windshield of the car, which acted as a mirror in the blackness of the night. The taxi dropped us off in front of an illuminated entrance sheltered from the rain by a white canopy. The Padre rung at the imposing metallic door that bore a copper plaque with the words "Apocryphe—Private Club." A mesh spy-hole half-opened, then rapidly closed again. A woman opened the door only enough for us to enter, and then shut it sharply behind us. I couldn't distinguish anything at first, passing from the flood of light in the entrance to the shadows of the antechamber.

A staircase that subsequently I would descend countless times led past the cloakroom and into the club itself. There the maître d' sat us at a table in the corner, next to a staircase leading to the dance floor. From this table we had an almost complete overview of the club without the music deafening us, as it would have done one or two rows closer to the floor. The Padre introduced me to the manager, who came to greet us. He brought us a bottle along with two glasses and some orange juice, which he liked to add to his whiskey. This first time I didn't have the leisure I would have liked to observe the play of lights, the movements and appearances of the people there. The powerful booming of the loud speakers made it so that I had to lean in as closely as possible to hear and to be heard. And the conversation I had that night with the Padre, if I no longer remember it, swept along like so many others I had under similar circumstances, was absorbing enough that I only rarely raised my head. I retain only a fragmentary impression of this first night at the Apocryphe—my first experience at a place like this—as of a city faithfully reconstructed after a bombardment, pieced together from the testimony of photographs. Lights and music of such intensity that space and time were no longer coherent, lacerated and turned upside down in what seemed to be complete chaos. The countless mirrors that went as high as the ceiling and covered even the walls and pillars multiplied dimensions and bodies, preventing me from defining and pinpointing the effects I was feeling and turning the Apocryphe into a topographical enigma.

· · · · · · · · · · · · · · ·

I wasn't long in returning there, always in the company of the Padre, who I shadowed in all of his nocturnal outings. In April and May he almost exclusively frequented the Apocryphe, sometimes as often as four nights per week. He would call me at night around nine o'clock, always asking me if I was free and telling me to meet him there. I don't know what brought about this sudden intimacy; the substance of our relationship boiled down to club conversations, not quite the conversations of confidants. Retrospectively, I think perhaps he was hoping for a more intimate liaison, but falling in love with me would have posed him too many problems. Maybe he secretly desired that I would be the one to initiate a declaration he didn't dare make.

One night in May, we were seated at our usual table discussing the performance of *Don Giovanni* we had just seen at the Opéra when George, the manager of the club, came looking for us. He led us along the dance floor toward the bathroom. There, lying on the floor, his head in a pool of blood, the DJ was dying. Next to the toilet were a little blackened spoon and a syringe still containing a bit of murky liquid. George had had this part of the bathroom closed to the public; we pulled the almost lifeless body toward the sinks, leaving a wake of blood. Michel—that was the DJ's name—must have fallen, cracking his skull open against the edge of the toilet bowl or on the ground. In the harsh light of the room we discerned what the faint, colored luminosity of the club had always masked: a deathly pale complexion, skin like plaster, eyes sunken in their sockets and circled with bluish rings. The pronounced marks of cyanosis were visible on his face. The raised sleeve of his shirt revealed an arm marbled with old injection scars. His heart was beating faintly, stopping then restarting. The Padre asked if anyone had called an ambulance. George frowned at the question: he had looked for a doctor among the clientele and, not having found one, had fallen back on a priest. To inform the police of such an incident would be all they needed to close down the club. The Padre tried to do a few chest compressions before quickly giving up. He began to recite a summary of the Extreme Unction, continuing even when a final jerk produced a grimace that revealed rotting teeth in Michel's death-kissed mouth. The squalidness of the setting, of this demise concocted between dirty water, white powder, and a suspicious syringe, was making me nauseous. The stench of vile shit was invading my nostrils. I bumped into a bottle of vodka that was lying there for no reason; it spilled over the ground where it shattered, mixing its contents with the blood pooled nearby. It was then that I noticed the flies that had come from who knows where to swarm above the puddle.

The Padre and the manager, kneeling on either side of the corpse, said nothing. Although the bathroom was secluded from the club, the imperturbable thuds of the bass still reached us in a mumble. We had to decide the fate of this corpse relatively quickly so that no one would suspect anything. Only Elvire, the bathroom attendant, was abreast of the situation. When she noticed that Michel—whom she had suspected was taking drugs—hadn't come out of the bathroom in a long time, she sensed some kind of accident and alerted the manager, who, forcing open the door, had discovered his DJ in the aforementioned state. Memories of similar scenes in novels popped uselessly into our heads. George was still refusing to alert the police and the Padre was reluctantly starting to agree. The law, other than divine law, mattered little to him, and a dead body was a dead body; the tribulations of a corpse had no influence on the destiny of its soul, now liberated. Michel wasn't leaving behind a widow or an orphan, he had no known relations. Such is the heroic life of a junkie: cruising and seclusion. He had started working there only recently, receiving money under the table.

What were we to do? Seal off this part of the bathroom under the pretext of a leak and, in the morning, once the clientele and personnel had left, transport the corpse to his house and abandon it there? We would only be shifting the location of the incident; the evidence of Michel's vice would do the rest. But carrying out the operation posed some risks. And a police investigation that was even the slightest bit thorough would have found George and the Padre guilty of paying an employee under the table, failing to assist a person in danger, concealing a corpse, false witnessing, and who knows what else. I would be implicated too, most likely.

Only one solution remained: we had to get rid of this corpse that no one was coming to claim, adding Michel to the list of those vanished without a trace. But where would we put the body? The Seine, that perilous solution, was too far away. All three of us, standing around the corpse, were staring at it and trying to think. Suddenly I spotted a groove in the ground that demarcated the edges of a plaque, partially covered by the corpse. I had been staring at it for a long time without really noticing it. Finally, I asked what it was. It was the entrance to the septic tank and the pump that allowed its contents to flow into the sewer. We moved the corpse onto its side and lifted it up. The tank, commensurate with the size of the club, was big enough for us to imagine hiding a body there. But we had to be careful to avoid blocking the opening of the pump once the corpse was inside, which would hinder its functioning and draw unwanted attention. The motor and its opening were situated at one end of the tank. We had to let the corpse float to the other end and then weigh it down so that it wouldn't drift. The operation, simple in theory, was more complicated in execution: it was out of the question that one of us would go wading in this cesspool; so we had to calculate accurately, and in one stroke thrust the corpse into just the right spot.

First we searched his pockets, removing his wallet and the keys to his car and apartment. George would get rid of any form of identification, move his car from where it was parked behind the Apocryphe, and purge Michel's house of any clue capable of compromising the establishment. We sent Elvire for some floor rags and a broom. We still needed an object that would weigh the body down to the bottom of this pool of sludge and keep it there. George went to the end of the hallway and opened the door to the cellar where he fetched, concealed in a bucket, a cinder block left over from some construction job in the club, and a synthetic fiber cord that was used during parties as a clinch to suspend lanterns and other decorations. Then it was time to strip the corpse of its clothes, because they too risked hampering the functioning of the pump if they were to drift. We took off his shirt, shoes, socks, pants, even his briefs, which were soaked with urine from the *post mortem* loosening of the sphincters. They were all thrown in a heap near the sink, later to be torn into little pieces and collected in a plastic bag. The body, now naked, was stretched on the tiles, revealing the extent of the disaster brought on by drug abuse. He was skinny; high doses of heroine had shriveled his body, as if burning it from the inside. On all of his limbs, the injection scars—violet, yellow, or black depending on how recent they were—tattooed the Harlequin's costume onto his flesh. The blood that had oozed from his head wound was now nearly coagulated, glued in his blond hair, forming a brown scab upon his scalp. I caught the Padre with his eyes fixed on the dead man's penis and he diverted his gaze. George and I fastened the cinder block in place around Michel's waist with a dozen twists of the fine string. The dead man's eyes, which we had forgotten to close, were regarding me with no regard for me. Their empty fixity wasn't what troubled me, but the weight, in my arms, of this dead body. We each grabbed one end of the corpse. We slid it forward through the opening into the tank, holding onto it until the last second. Then, giving it a strong horizontal push, we let it go. The density of the tank's contents made it bob for a few moments, sliding before finally sinking. It was swallowed up from the center, under the weight of the cinder block that compressed its abdomen; the legs and arms disappeared last, absorbed as if regretfully by the malodorous mix of excrement and filth. I didn't have the wits about me to recite a *de profundis*. I stood up after letting the slab fall back into place and washed my hands. George and the Padre were attempting to clean the floor of all traces of the incident. I made the spoon and the syringe disappear down the toilet; they went to rejoin their worshipper. In a bag, the Padre collected the dead man's old rags, now reduced to shreds. George threw them deep into a trashcan, where they would soon be buried under the mass of putrescence produced by a night of partying.

In two weeks' time there would be no memory of the person who had manned the turntables at the Apocryphe; someone else would have taken his place, running the same ship with the same consenting slaves. We left the bathroom after asking Elvire to exercise the greatest discretion as to what she had seen. Whether the manager won her silence through money or threats, I don't know, but she kept quiet. We verified that Michel owed nothing at the coat check and we circulated the rumor that, feeling ill, he had asked the manager for permission to leave and had slipped out the fire exit, where he had parked his car. He didn't have any friends at the Apocryphe; the effect of heroin on his behavior had left him alienated, and consequently no one inquired about what had become of him. For the duration of the incident, a pre-recorded tape had covered for the missing DJ. However, things couldn't continue like this for the rest of the night.

George accompanied me to the DJ booth, a sort of podium that loomed over the dance floor. This glass-enclosed den was attached to one of the walls of the club, which was organized around it in concentric levels, making it the focal point. There were two lateral staircases leading to the back. George knew only the elementary principles of using the equipment, which he demonstrated to me succinctly, leaving it to me to break the code of how to properly manipulate the sound. He abandoned me there; now I was to reign over these fifteen square meters, cluttered with records and devices. It was my duty to make the crowd dance, those four hundred-something people who were in the club on that Friday night.

Never in my life had I done anything even remotely similar to what was suddenly demanded of me. Nothing that could have guided me came to mind. To manipulate the sound effects of a nightclub is quite different from putting some records on a stereo system. George left me with these extremely comforting words: "If you can't figure it out, if you panic, put on a tape. The important thing is that everyone see there's someone in this booth, and that there be no gaps in the music." So I let the tape play on while I attempted to train myself in the technique and to find my bearings in the stock of records stacked in the crates and bins all around me. A record was spinning on one of the turntables, about to come to an end; Michel must have put it on before going to the bathroom to inject himself one last time. On the other turntable, at a standstill with the arm posed on the first grooves of a track, the record that he had most likely prepared for his return was waiting. With my index finger I took the arm of the first turntable and set it back at the beginning of the record. Grabbing the headphones, I listened to the track, then, moving the fader, I did the same with the second. I was trying to figure out the principle of logical succession in the sequence he had planned—his only will and testament. In more than a month of coming to the Apocryphe, not once had I paid attention to the way the music transitioned. It had been a blanket without a snag; I had noticed no rip or seam. But I did remember the melody of the record I was now listening to in the headphones;

I had heard it numerous times but, I now realized, not all the way through. At the precise moment when a voice interrupted the melody, another track was usually overlaid. Which one or which ones, I wasn't sure; I didn't know any of the song titles.

It was two-thirty in the morning. I still had to fill the silence with noise for at least another three hours. Half-instinctively, half-methodically, I armed myself with a sheet of paper and started to explore the stock of records, trying to figure out how they had been organized. It seemed that the old records were arranged in the crates to my left and to my right, and the even older ones were under the turntables at my feet. I deduced their age by the state of their covers, a hypothesis I verified rapidly by pulling out four or five at random to find their copyright date. The records I found behind me, arranged facing out in the bins—probably to allow for rapid consultation—seemed to be the most recent. A more thorough examination of this part of the record collection revealed that it was constituted mostly of what are known in the business as "extended versions," the maxi singles that offer one sole track on their two sides in different versions—vocal mix, instrumental mix, or remix. At first I didn't discern any principle of order, but gradually concluded that they must have been put in a chronological, almost geological, stockpile following when they were released, since, when I listened to them, one after another came slow and then fast rhythms of different, if not contradictory, genres. I listened briefly but attentively to about thirty records in a quarter of an hour, forming a basic outline of classification. I had never studied music; the few violin lessons that my grandmother had given me were of little use—I had been loath to learn traditional musical notation and so my studies had come to a quick end, lacking any foundation. The music I listened to at home or at concerts was completely different from what I had to tackle then. The sequence of the initial list I was compiling was founded in what I perceived instinctively in the thuds of the bass in each of the tracks. What I was able to observe of the dance floor compelled me to think that the dancers' movements revolved around these inaudible resonances shaking the floor beneath their feet. The tape that was playing while I was honing my technique confirmed my intuition. I tried a few times to identify the right moment to move from one record to another, and soon the essence of this transition became obvious to me.

The end of the tape was approaching. I put the two records Michel had left back on the turntables, restarting the musical continuity where it had been abandoned, and eased my way into the vast wave of rhythm carrying these bodies. On the mixer, for each turntable, there was a corresponding volume fader with its own equalizer—midrange and treble. I cued the first track on the turntable and sent the signal through the amplifiers and loudspeakers while gradually fading out the music from the tape recorder. I learned to repeat the same transition about every five minutes; the rhythm of my night was decided not by the music itself but by the necessity of its unfailing continuity. I didn't have anyone to teach me this art form, but my approach, although it entailed quite a bit of initial fumbling, guaranteed a methodical manner that I later noticed many DJs lack.

I must have done a decent job; at the end of the night, George relayed the compliments people had made to him about me. In the implicit comparison with the deceased, whom people believed had left on a whim, I came out on top. People asked who I was, where I had come from, where I had previously been mixing, and George told them that one of his friends had brought me back in his suitcase from an underground club in Berlin where I had worked until now. As delighted as one can be with a corpse on his hands, he proposed that I continue the next day and, since the university's vacation was coming up, that I take over the position for the three months of summer if I had nothing better to do. He gave me the five hundred francs that normally went to Michel and asked me to make a decision by the next day.

Around six in the morning, as I was starting to acquire a taste for my new post, he told me to stop the music. The club emptied of its last clients. In one corner the personnel were dividing up the tips collected during the night and receiving their allocated percentage on each beverage served. George stayed, along with the Padre and me, to turn off the lights and the amplifiers and to close the doors. The Padre, passing by the bathroom, made an ironic comment in allusion to the resurrections sprinkled throughout the Bible. Leaving the darkness of the Apocryphe, the light of day hurt my eyes. That sleepless night left me in a stupor. George went to execute the final steps of our plan. He left the Padre and me at the edge of the sidewalk with the following words: "God be with us!" The invocation wasn't funny but it made me smile. I looked at the Padre; the morning sun bathing his face made it seem even paler. He thanked me for my help. The Padre confided in me later that George was one of his closest friends: they had spent two years studying together in a Jesuit college where the cream of the Madrid bourgeoisie sent their children. They had lost touch, reconnecting by chance years later in a Paris nightclub…He recounted the story of their friendship for me without ever explaining what had made them so close. In any case, all three of us henceforth were linked by a corpse. We separated at the taxi stand on Avenue Matignon and agreed to meet up later that night.

· · · · · · · · · · · · · ·

And so began what seemed to me a new life, but what seemed to all those who knew me the beginning of a resigned and aimless wandering. The Padre neither encouraged nor discouraged me from this new path; after all, he had been partly responsible for leading me into it. That day we chatted on the phone, neither of us bringing up the morbid events of the night before except in terms of the possible negative consequences on my future. But I had become indifferent to my fate. A possibility, an opportunity even, was presenting itself, and I was abandoning myself to it, following an inclination that the naïve might call "natural." I acquiesced to whatever presented itself without much arm-twisting, and I neither suffered from nor reveled in it: I was spared the exhaustion of searching and seizing. I was giving up a state of being that was in turn abandoning me and sliding into another that slowly, imperceptibly came to envelop me.

Around six that night, I took a shower and dressed myself with an unusual attentiveness. I went out to eat in a little restaurant located on the slope of Montmartre. The little old lady who tended the stoves was very fond of me. Ever since I had found myself without any family ties, I had taken up the habit of dining in this restaurant frequented only by those of the neighborhood. Jeanne and her husband served a cuisine that was certainly lacking in refinement but that I found nostalgic, and I was in that sort of mood. Seated at a table with a very worn plastic tablecloth, my mind was racing: ideas and images were strung together in a film of uncertain speed, poorly montaged, often skipping and shifting. I pushed myself back in my chair and absent-mindedly played with the food left on my plate. Jeanne came over, worried that I hadn't eaten enough. She sat down in the chair opposite me and wiped her hands on her black cotton apron. Faintly wheezing from her asthma, she stared at me without wanting to disrupt my daydreaming, waiting for me to confess the secrets she saw in my eyes. But I didn't know where to begin, or how to recount the change happening in my life. Suddenly I smiled at her. She praised my unusual elegance, feeling the silk of my shirt. For the first time she saw the mark of the bourgeoisie on me. I had pulled these clothes from the bottom of an armoire where they had been relegated after I wore them for a series of flashy events that crop up in certain phases of life, those moments of urbane frivolity when one is suddenly caught up in a frenzied succession of parties, receptions, and salons. Jeanne was secretly admiring me in this outfit; it looked like something a posh person would wear. It was if I were eclipsing the modesty of her small café and the old-fashioned simplicity of her clothes with this intrusion of refinement. She commented on my appearance, highlighting with a sort of possessive avidity how nicely a classic haircut would accentuate my facial features. Then I explained the cause of this grand display.

Jeanne had an outdated idea of high society: she both feared nocturnal adventures and admired this newfound luxury, this idea of a life of partying that only old money or the *nouveau riche* could afford. The difference between a nightclub like the Apocryphe and a cabaret or shady dive on the Place Pigalle remained obscure for her. She saw how easy it was to pass from socialite to has-been, from night owl to washed-up, and she feared for me a fate worse than death and its torments. She got up to make me a coffee. I lingered for another hour after having finished dinner. Then, after a kiss from Jeanne on the forehead, I made my way down the hill, taking my time on the most indirect roads.

After this nocturnal drifting through deserted streets, I arrived on time at the Apocryphe. A number of people were coming out of impressive cars and rushing to the entrance. The door opened onto violent light and red shadows dancing on a wide staircase illuminated by projector beams, provoking a feeling of disoriented wandering, as if my identity had been lost or dissolved within the chiaroscuro. Passing through the entrance of the club, something of my being was lost or absorbed, an inexplicable and immeasurable stripping away that, once I finally ended up on the dance floor, hadn't left any of me behind except my carnal covering, spurred on only by the rhythmic pulsing of the music. Confronted with the bass,

I was seized by a contraction; on the other extreme, a sharp trepan bore into my skull. The effect dulled once one had grown accustomed to it but continued to operate nevertheless. My body wore itself out with retractions of fleeting deliverance.

That second night I put into practice and observed the effects of the principles I had managed to deduce the night before. I stopped focusing on mere manual technique and instead focused on the reactions of the dance floor to this or that experimental effect. There I had free rein to try my hand at this new expertise. I was captivated by the idea of a struggle with no stakes other than my own satisfaction. I was experimenting without any restrictions, embarking upon the basics of a new language that no one had taught me; I was the master and the student, but the apprenticeship of this new science was not a form of autodidacticism. Rather, I was discovering the rules as I went along, establishing what had always existed without any basic precepts. Each night I was giving a speech in this unknown, unformulated language, unaware that I was deviating from a specific practice that so many others had followed before me.

George and the Padre came to see me each in his turn while I was working. In that glassed-in booth, a visit felt like an invasion. We chatted, cramped together, our words masked by the music, obscured behind a wall of sound. They both noticed that I displayed a magnificent and unexpected gift for the task at hand. It was settled that until I found another job I would remain the resident DJ. The Padre couldn't help acting as a sort of moral guide—he had decided to view this adventure as an ablution, as a necessary submersion in the world of terrestrial passions. It was a type of trial, a confrontation with the excesses of evil designed to steel my character.

· · · · · · · · · · · · · · ·

My memory of all this is broken, incomplete. All those nights ended up melting into one, jerky and repetitive like the music I was distilling there in a state of extreme fatigue. I had never stuck with anything long enough to really immerse myself in it. Ennui was my curse and nothing was ever able to shake me out of it. The strangeness lurking beneath the surface of something could only last for so long. Everything quickly became a tainted repetition, void of all charm. Faced with this flesh I was trying to make move every night, I felt disgust, a brutal alternating between excitement and dejection, resulting in surrender to my essential melancholy. All I felt was contempt, such intense contempt! The numerous, innumerable bodies made up a monster of a hundred heads and tangled limbs whose only cohesion and life force came from the rhythmic impulse I dealt to it. The whole night, an absurd imperative commanded me to postpone the inevitable death and division of this collective body that I was making evolve before my eyes, from my glass booth shaking it with charges of sound and bombarding it with lightning. I thought about my work—admittedly mortal and ephemeral—with fear, the fear of a demiurge caught in the position of damned hero, who finds a brother in Sisyphus. The fear of God when He realizes, without having foreseen it, that His first act has now made Him a slave of continuous Creation. God cursing when He realizes that without His knowledge, He has been made the driving engine of the morbid embraces crossing this panicked body born of Him, of His sweat, of His strained efforts and His unarticulated cries. A dizzying disgust would take hold of me as I overcame the inertia of these separate bodies, still reluctant to come together.

However, I did experience nights of rapture that no human ecstasy can equal, those nights when, for some unknown reason, a sort of inspired fury seized the entire club. This trancelike state that I provoked and prolonged vibrated through my body and carried me to unimaginable excesses of delirium. One such night is still carved into my memory, a Saturday in October—coincidentally also my birthday. The party lasted well beyond the usual timeframe. Strictly speaking, I was no longer listening to the music; it was passing through me. I was cuing up the records as if by instinct, my vision obscured by a veil of blood. I was in a coma agitated by rhythms that were more and more painfully arousing my desire without ever draining it. In a vague fog I discerned the compact mass of people dancing, flattened one against the other and yet swaying, lifted up in waves. United almost without fissure, they were probably incapable of moving, but the entire mass vibrated in rhythm, all individual drives undone and lost in a higher, sovereign need. George told me later that everyone who entered the club mixed gradually into this mob and that between the hours of two and six in the morning nobody left, the employees were overwhelmed. At eight in the morning, emptied, I collapsed onto a bench and went to sleep.

That night sealed my reputation. It still reigns supreme in my memory; no other night ever achieved such furious intensity. From then on they all seemed bland and nondescript. That night inflicted a violence upon me, an annihilation; I experienced what only sex at its extremes allows one to feel, infrequently and fleetingly. I had reached a limit, and after that came repetition and ennui.

I was guided by habit, or maybe addiction, as I left my house every night around midnight. I no longer slept at night; what had previously been a tendency of mine became a permanent mode of being. Anxiety would propel me into the streets and at nightfall, as if mechanically, I would get dressed to go out. The pallor of my complexion was heightened; in the light of day I looked like a corpse. Moreover, the sun's glare hurt my eyes, so I started to avoid it.

Even when I didn't have to serve as DJ at the Apocryphe, I would go out to other clubs where I was always let in because people recognized me.

I would check out half a dozen, ending up each morning in the club that stayed open the latest, frequented by a mostly black clientele. I dawdled in all the places that were in vogue at the time. My eclecticism pushed me to ignore differences and transgress against exclusions; I entered indiscriminately into clubs that were gay or straight, male or female. I didn't mind whether the place was a notorious dive or a hideaway of respectable sharks. By nature rather silent and reserved, whether from a sense of privacy or from my convictions, I had little to fear from these drunken late-night wanderings through this beautiful world abandoned to vice. The exquisite correctness of my manners, the benevolent moderation I flaunted in every place and in every circumstance, made it so that I was easily accepted: the Mafiosi propping up the bars would offer me cigars and pat me warmly on the shoulder; the groomed, bejeweled women adored the air of dreamy adolescence still floating around me. The contrast between my young age and the maturity legible in my serious features was comforting; they were sure of my discretion and that sufficed in this milieu. I didn't drink much, which was astonishing to them. They never once saw me drunk but from the start I made known my high tolerance for alcohol, which they viewed as a strength; once this had been proven, I was able to stop drinking altogether, and they only respected me the more. I pretended that I was victim to gentle vices, the better to conceal my real vices, which would have seemed scandalous. They affectionately mocked me for my intellectual aura. I had to have a fault; they focused on this one and neglected to notice the others. This magnified aura made me feared, which is to say hated, by certain people, but at the same time, the distance that my intellectual reputation established kept me from dangerous familiarities. I spoke little and listened a lot: the ideal role, as so many people are in perpetual search of an indulgent ear for their nighttime rants. The sum of the stories they confided in me could fill entire volumes of sociological or ethnological reports. There was the tedious and nonsensical conversation of tipsy society men; the chatter vaguely colored with the philosophy and aestheticism of the washed-up who cling to a completely superficial and secondhand culture as a fiery temper clings to a menopausal *bourgeoise*; and, in passing, the virile and noxious conversations of old bachelors following the antics of their protégées out of the corner of their eyes—I was subjected to it all, and I listened with all the presence of mind that was still within my power in those hours of confusion.

What was I looking for there? A distraction from an imperceptible anguish? The response to a question I hadn't yet formulated? Evasion? Flight? I don't even know. But it became a game for me to go out like this. Entering a club or a bar was in a way like going to the cinema: a dark room with sounds and images in three dimensions (were there really three?). I lived on the film set of an enormous stock of unrealized B-movies of a hitherto unseen genre. At the hour when the television programs come to an end, when the last spectators leave from the theaters and the marquees are taken down, a different vision appears, a variation each night on the same miserable and violent scenario.

II

My new lifestyle wasn't immediately upended by meeting A★★★. I merely added a preliminary stop to my nights—an obligatory visit to the Eden. However, my fascination, quickly transforming into passion, soon required more. To satisfy it, I had to start making more than one daily courtesy call.

A★★★ loved going out to clubs once the show at the Eden was over. Soon after, some of the other dancers from the Eden, dragged in A★★★'s wake, would show up at the Apocryphe. They did me the honor of dancing to the music I played and their performance gave me a new enthusiasm for my work. At certain moments throughout the night A★★★ would come keep me company in my glass booth, dancing until the surroundings were eclipsed, leaning in to say something to me with an accent I found irresistible. A★★★'s spirit, like A★★★'s dance, was infused with a crafty and charming naïveté.

Soon we became rather close; we would call each other almost every day when we woke up and would eat dinner together at least once a week, just the two of us, after which I would allow myself to escort A★★★ to the Eden. We would meet again at the Apocryphe, and would often go loiter somewhere else after closing. This strange intimacy didn't stem from any common social or intellectual interests; it wasn't the sign or effect of a close friendship or romantic relationship. I wasn't particularly enthralled by the originality of A★★★'s views, or by a similarity in our tastes; we neither combated nor conversed. Our time together and our conversation were simply a pleasure, like the contemplation of A★★★'s body or A★★★'s dance, an aesthetic pleasure that I could attribute only to a lightness of being that never dipped into inanity. I can't define A★★★ as being anything other than both frivolous and serious, residing in the subtle dimension of presence without insistence.

Our arrival together at every locale and the attention we paid to each other started to incite gossip. Our encounters, which took place only in public, aroused suspicions of a private affair that, at the time, didn't exist. At the Apocryphe and everywhere we went, people made remarks about our striking dissimilarity. They teased me over the contrast in color between our skins, they stressed the difference in our mannerisms: the impulsiveness of A★★★'s voice and gestures, that wild exuberance and openness to the world, which by comparison underscored my moderation and reserve. A★★★ in turn had to bear the incessant prattle about my religious and social background. They painted a picture of my incomprehensible oddities: my isolation; my taste for solitude strangely coexisting with a sudden dive into this world; an unheralded abandon of a university career for the improvised post of DJ. For want of any intelligible coherence, they assumed I must have been harboring some kind of vice or perversion.

What did I get out of spending all my time with someone with whom I shared no social, intellectual, or racial community? That was precisely the question troubling them. Black skin, white skin: our looks were against us. Our intimacy went against the mandate dictating that birds of a feather flock together. And this impossible clash of colors produced the general opinion that this was an unnatural union.

In order to stop the scandal, we diluted our dissimilarity by always hanging out in a group. But the people in this crowd tried to detach me from A★★★ by attempting to convince me that we were fundamentally incompatible. I couldn't care less that my attachment to my seemingly perfect antithesis was provoking worry and alarm. They complained of A★★★'s numerous affairs, highlighted A★★★'s notorious fickleness and capriciousness that would make any real attachment impossible. They charitably forewarned me that I wasn't A★★★'s "type," that we weren't even of the same species. That if my intention was to turn this friendship into something more, it was best to give up now, and that if, by some misfortune, it had already become something more, it was just as well to break it off now before it dissolved into unpleasantries and pain.

I thoroughly did not care about their opinions, their advice and warnings, their slanders and denigrations. I was well aware of A★★★'s fickleness, capriciousness, and quickly changing tastes, for I had witnessed all of these traits myself. As for this concert of well-intentioned deceit and charitable denunciations aimed at discouraging me, I was deaf to it all.

· · · · · · · · · · · · · ·

One morning at the Kormoran, that final stopover for night owls, an old mobster whom I knew and liked rather more than his congeners saw me enter with A★★★, called me over to his usual spot at the bar, and, after the customary ceremonious greetings, imparted this strange speech, interspersed with knowing winks:

"You know me. I like you. So listen up. All those idiots, they don't know anything. Because they see us chatting fairly often and because I seem to know you pretty well, for a week now they've been coming to me to complain that you're mucking around, that you're out of your mind. That you're foolishly running after that attractive animal there [gesturing toward A★★★]. You know what they say to me? That it could never work between whites and blacks...And that, furthermore, you two aren't compatible...That one's always dancing, you're always hitting the books. They come to me desperately seeking an explanation...

[He paused to finish his whiskey] But they've got it all wrong, I'm telling you...I've been observing your conquest for two weeks now...And I know what blacks are like...For ten years I've been watching them pass through here...Listen to me: if you keep at it, you will succeed...All those assholes are talking bullshit...Saying that you're lowering yourself! That's what they've been saying to you, right? When you talk to them, they don't absorb anything, and so they can't understand what you see in A★★★...[He ordered another drink and relit his cigar] But I get what you see...Come back to me in a month and we'll discuss it again. Because it's not at all a lost cause, it just takes a bit of time. Yeah? Turn on the charm! Bring out the violins and *tutti quanti*...It takes time, but you can handle it...Have patience, and by God, you will succeed! And they'll have to eat their words."

He firmly grasped my hand after finishing his speech, pronounced in his eternally hoarse voice, rolling the gravel of an accent that rendered him incomprehensible to any ear unaccustomed to the deformations he inflicted on his syllables. The high-end escort keeping him company winked while watching me with a slightly alarmed air. Ruggero, as he called himself, was studying me paternally, a cigar wedged between his teeth, gauging my surprise. "Persevere or you'll have me to deal with... When you achieve your victory, the champagne is on me. Don't let yourself be intimidated by the blathering, the scandals, and the bullshit... Now go tend to your love affair."

I went and found A★★★, who had no clue about the sermon I had just endured. No doubt others had taken advantage of those ten minutes I had spent with Ruggero to make remarks about how I seemed to want to capture A★★★'s attention, and more still, at any price. They saw us everywhere together, but no act or gesture allowed them to definitively conclude it had turned into an affair. They didn't know what to believe, and for them that was insufferable. They would have excused a brisk adventure, without consequence and without tomorrow—what was called in this milieu "getting some ass." But an attachment that appeared to stem from something other than sex was intolerable.

Ruggero had, however, clumsily formulated what I had been struggling to express myself, without it being, on my part, a conscious project or concerted maneuver. His soliloquy had clarified and simplified the ideas floating around in my head. Indeed, I'm sure that had been his aim. What I was feeling for A★★★ needed its own embodiment; the pleasure I took in A★★★'s company demanded its own fulfillment. I wanted A★★★, it was true, and all my other desires, needs, and plans paled in comparison. Suddenly, the obsessive clamor for amorous possession took hold of me.

I was surprised to find myself desiring, painfully. In a sudden rush of vertigo, I was tantalized by the idea of contact with A★★★'s skin. I wanted to dismiss, destroy all those who were thronging around A★★★, keeping this presence from me. I wanted to wrest A★★★ from their company, from the intrusive glances clinging to us there, and hide us both away. With an unknowingly crazed look, I was always watching this irresistible body. But my gaze was narrowing and stiffening under the tension of carnal desire. That night, A★★★ was wearing a black silk shirt and white pleated leather pants that showed off a firm behind. A★★★'s hair, shaved not long ago for the show, was beginning to grow back, materializing as a light shadow. That face, thus restored to its pure nudity, appeared without interference, without anything that could deceptively modify its proportions or veil its imperfections. Its features had retained nothing of A★★★'s African origins, except for a barely perceptible, sensual heaviness of the mouth.

I don't know what more to say about this body, although I spent hours contemplating it. But that night, my contemplation was exorbitant, quickly twisting into a desire to take possession…A★★★ noticed my unusual comportment. I made excuses; I didn't dare reveal the reason for my turmoil and so I was restraining myself from clearly expressing my feelings. I spent the end of that night in a state of incredible confusion: daggers of desire, scattered snippets of conversation, a fragmented vision of A★★★ dancing were all assailing me in a blur.

We separated on a street corner with the light kiss on the lips that wasn't reserved for me alone. Once home, I was unable to fall asleep, although the night had been, per usual, long and draining. But the exhaustion, which, in the stages of desire, typically follows confused excitation, emptied me of all energy, of even that energy required to sleep. I was turning over in my bed as one might collapse onto a body in the heat of a furious embrace. I was tortured by the memory of A★★★'s scent, by the residual imprint, barely there, of a shoulder resting against my own this morning as we spoke. The ghost of A★★★'s presence against mine; a hand poised for a moment on my face, our thighs pressed together in a cramped space. I had the sensation in my flesh of contact with those limbs, no longer there; the effect lingered long after its source had disappeared, retaining the same intensity. A hallucinatory sensation, as if my body had suffered an amputation. This sensation that, even after the split, the separation of our two bodies kept scalding me, kept me awake. I oscillated the entire morning between the rage of embracing only a void, and the memory, the bliss of an instant, of the past night that I was trying so hard mentally to recompose.

Around two in the afternoon, I got out of bed without having slept, prey to a mixture of despair and exhaustion. Wandering the apartment aimlessly, the shutters closed, I declaimed in an incoherent monologue all that passed through my head for the next two hours. The sound of the telephone, which rang right in the middle of my vociferations, terrified me. I knew who was calling, but I was afraid of answering and betraying my nervousness. Nonetheless, I answered it and managed to control myself for long enough to agree to meet A★★★ around six o'clock at the Café de Flore.

As soon as we hung up, I hurriedly started getting ready. In the shower, I promised myself twenty times that I would declare my passion that night in no uncertain terms, which I immediately began to assemble and articulate. Looking at myself in the mirror, I swore when I saw the bags under my eyes, which were much worse than usual. Then I wasted a good twenty minutes wondering what clothes to wear on this solemn occasion; I wanted to look my best, which, normally, was the least of my concerns. Look good! Look good! The idea suddenly made me shrug. I observed my naked form displayed in the mirror: was it really that important how I chose to veil my nudity? Since I had lost weight (the mirror confirmed this), my clothes, which I always wore a bit loose, had become rather baggy. I surveyed my wardrobe, still unable to decide what to wear. In a sudden fury to be done with this inner debate on the uselessness of artifice, I grabbed the first pair of pants and the first shirt to fall into my hands. I pulled on my usual leather jacket and left in a rush from the apartment, dreading a late arrival to this decisive rendezvous.

· · · · · · · · · · · · · ·

Before A★★★ brought me there, I had never stepped foot in the Café de Flore. I held a sort of prejudice against this place that stemmed from an old image of the 1950s to which it was for me indissolubly linked. My aversion to this distressing, foul-smelling intellectualism—also known as "existentialism"—was combined with my distrust of these clichéd spaces where public notoriety summons a hybrid species of artists and intellectuals. That they packed together there didn't imply that the place was in good taste; quite the opposite, their presence foretold an undeniable unpleasantness.

Contrary to the theological idea that if I value the Creator very highly,

I can't admire His creation or honor His creature, when a work of art moved me to the highest point I could only comparatively disparage the author once he or she was relegated to the dismal banality of this café.

To mix with company that derives its life force from the desire to show off is to confine oneself to the enslavement of the ogler; I was disgusted by this pagan and idolatrous Mass, its adepts, its servants, and its totems. And so when I crossed the threshold of this temple for the first time, I wasn't surrendering to its obscene cult, but to desire alone, and to the deliberate invitation of A★★★ who, living close by, enjoyed tanning on the terrace in the summer. The perverse effect of A★★★'s presence was the only thing that made this café tolerable. A★★★'s tendency to constantly act as if on a stage relegated me to the wings or to the coatroom, which suited me perfectly. As soon as I infiltrated the Flore, I reduced myself to being nothing but a sort of understudy; and only this rather particular statute, which exempted me from the widespread and monstrous fury of recognition, allowed me to show myself without showing off myself.

That evening, without a glance at the audience, I steered myself toward a table tucked to the side where I always insisted on sitting, and where A★★★ was waiting for me. The proclamations that I had debated nonstop en route crystallized unexpectedly at the sight of A★★★, and I abruptly broached the subject close to my heart, as if to get it out of the way. A declaration of love is always tedious; it exceeded my patience to dilute the exasperation of my passion in a detailed statement, to represent discursively the unbearable confusion of my immediate desire— tolerating neither delay nor explanation, so much did its urgency torment me. My intentions were clear; my speech only muddled and veiled them in incoherence. I was alternating aimlessly between snippets of narration, the minutes of my interior monologue, syllogisms and images, passing without transition from slang to high style and from the trivial to the abstract, without ever finding the right tone or genre in which to deliver my words. A★★★ was taken aback by this unprecedented bout of garrulous, confused violence.

A★★★'s response to the declaration I proved incapable of making was, however, perfectly clear. Its essence could be summarized with a single verdict: "You must not love me"—an attempt to claim that A★★★ was unworthy of my passion and that it would damage our friendship. A★★★'s propensity had always been to refrain from passionate attachments of the flesh, attachments that, once broken by misfortune, betrayal, or accident, resulted in prejudicial excesses of sadness. Consequently, A★★★ thought it wise to disavow the idea of amorous possession, which could do nothing but exacerbate my confusion and forbid us from returning thereafter to that honest friendship, that guarantee of stability, to which we would be better off confining ourselves.

That response, the arguments used to justify A★★★'s refusal, were attempts to disorient me; in fact they did nothing but accentuate even more the imperative violence of my desire. They also left room for debate. All of the notions of love A★★★'s reasoning invoked seemed erroneous to me, and I set about proving it. Those reasons were only a pretext; I wanted the truth. I was ranting, using cunning to obtain it, and seeing that the facts were being concealed from me, I brazenly concluded that they must have been in my favor. We spent the night discussing, disputing the erroneous fables used to justify A★★★'s refusal, and the valid reasons for my desire. Through every tone I modulated the absolute demand and legitimacy of my passion.

In return, A★★★ took refuge behind a moderation far from the habitual impulsiveness to which I was accustomed. That night the inversion was complete: I made myself into a demon, and A★★★ symmetrically put on the mask of the angel that I had abandoned. A★★★'s final argument, pronounced on the threshold of the Eden, was of this order: "I rely on your friendship, and a physical relationship would annihilate it irremediably; so you must not love me, for such a relationship would be hellish. Don't ask of me what I'm unable to give you without the risk of letting you down." I relate neither the exact terms of this plea—they were much more trivial—nor the precise progression of A★★★'s personal logic, which was much less clearly defined. And I cannot relate them simply because A★★★ never formulated a link between successive sentences. From an unorganized mass of statements, of partial notes and arguments, I managed to extract a line of reasoning, a collection of synthetic propositions that I subsequently reiterated to verify their accuracy. For example, the following assertions emitted more than an hour apart: "If I agree to sleep with you, things won't be the same afterward;" and, "I'm ill-tempered, no one tolerates me for long;" and, "We can't sleep together, we'll end up fighting because neither of us will want to let the other take the lead." I concluded implicitly that A★★★, only able to imagine love as a system of power relations, could only envisage our relationship as a battle, leading irremediably to a violent rupture. I had to translate and arrange every word so that they became intelligible to me. Add to this some misunderstandings stemming from different mother tongues, and perhaps one can grasp the difficulty of my enterprise.

This resistance, despite being hard to define, did not disarm me: I persevered and kept at it for weeks, trying to prove to A★★★ through every means imaginable that to succumb to my pleas and do the deed, far from destroying our affection, would only deepen and reinforce it. I insisted, tactically, on this shocking fact: A★★★'s not-so prudish attitude could coexist with my moral rigidity, and a carefree practice of bodily exhibition could rub shoulders with an equally strong contempt and suspicion of the flesh. In other words, that A★★★'s excesses could go hand in hand with my moderation and decorum. Far from being enraged by my obstinacy or taking offense at my incessant urging, A★★★ found it all quite amusing. This was a good sign. Certainly the variety of my pleas was astonishing; one often finds oneself suddenly capable of deploying the treasures of rhetoric, imagination, and persuasion in order to convince someone to have sex—a very common ambition, and not so interesting when one thinks about it in the cold light of day. But voilà, the price that I seemed to attach to my conquest, measured in terms of the energy and ingenuity I was expending, was high enough to be flattering. What must have seemed at first to be a passing blaze of concupiscence was, over time, taking on real form.

Our daily telephone conversations were no longer anything but a game: a hypothetical reconstruction of our relationship if A★★★ were to succumb to my desires. We were presenting each other with illusions, visions, and tableaux. The object of this display was to figure out how to get along without drama, how to deal with the overcrowding engendered by a relationship that we hoped would not be temporary, but rather truly invested with stable affections, tastes, habits, and lifestyles—all of which differed radically, even more each day. We discussed everything down to the most trivial details. Would we live together? And if so, how would we divide up the household chores? Would we sleep in separate beds, thus shielding ourselves from the boredom of a complacent conjugality? And if not, what type of bedding would we choose? A★★★ was pushing for the classic pairing of sheets and covers, I for the more rational duvet.

The slow workings of this fiction, which didn't shy away from any ridiculous or insignificant detail, were taking on the meticulous traits of familiarity. It was winning A★★★ over to the possibility of such a relation-ship. Its incongruity, its danger was dissipating in the soothing quietude of our constructed fable. Repetition and habit tend to diffuse excess. A★★★

was no longer systematically imagining the worst, no longer predicting disasters at every turn; the scenarios were becoming less catastrophic. Our union, by dint of simulation, was no longer completely inconceivable. The game of "and if" wore down A★★★'s reluctance; every day, we already belonged to each other in our imaginations. My desire was gaining power through a trick, was gaining life through a fiction.

Finally it no longer seemed to be a perilous trap to plan a vacation together, an idea I had secretly been entertaining for a long time now. I convinced A★★★ to go away with me to Munich for a few days just before Christmas, with no ulterior motive, in keeping with our "and if..." We left, pretending for a laugh that it was our honeymoon, where of course nothing scandalous would actually happen. One morning, after a night of work, we boarded the first plane for Munich and settled into a comfortable hotel room around noon.

The weather was astonishingly beautiful for the entire duration of our trip. A★★★, who had lived for some time in Munich, knew a lot of people there. I went along on some visits, but I saved three afternoons for myself to go from church to church and to make a rapid tour of some of the museums. It was important for me to prove to A★★★ that a relationship didn't amount to servitude and suffocation. Nevertheless, I was trying to secure the promise that we would visit the church Saint★★★ together, a little Baroque gem that I thought A★★★ would like because of its excessive decorative style and outrageous ornamental magnificence. Indeed, this extreme manifestation of Baroque taste, magnified in the confined proportions of that church, swallowed up and overwhelmed the view, from the spiral trompe-l'oeil to the horrible allusion to the confessional placed under the sign of the skull and crossbones.

Catholic and as far as possible from the censorious tastes of the Puritans, A★★★ was the perfect antithesis to white, Anglo-Saxon, Protestant

America. The spirit of the Counter-Reformation suited A★★★ perfectly, and, in guessing that, I had brought A★★★ a pleasure that might never have been discovered otherwise.

Munich also had some nightclubs to offer. Each night we visited three or four, where A★★★'s extensive notoriety was again made clear to me. Two years spent in Munich had sufficed to make A★★★ known in more or less all of the city's social circles. In each of these clubs, we were always invited to a table where I was introduced to a mob of people I would have been incapable of recognizing if I were to meet them again.

The clubs in Munich closed earlier than in Paris and some of them legally had to shut down at two o'clock. This particular policy forced us into a transhumance around four in the morning, inevitably leading us to a rather snooty club—the Sans-Nom, the Bavarian equivalent to the Apocryphe, frequented moreover by the same fashionable idlers that can be found in all the major cities of the world.

We would return by taxi to our hotel, which was not too far from the city center but still removed from the old town. The room had only one bed and we slept side by side in a platonic concubinage, as if this sort of asceticism were natural for us, or agreed upon in advance. There was a hint of perversity in this game; before I went to sleep I kept calculating all the possible consequences of transgressing. That A★★★ had conceded to come away with me and to share a bed with me, that sleeping next to each other had seemed to go without saying, could have been a sign that I had permission to succumb to the temptation currently putting my perseverance to the test. I was excited by the proximity of A★★★'s body; I didn't know whether to suppress this excitement or to give it free rein. What was it that A★★★ really desired? Each night, a ray of light, passing through the slightly opened curtains, illuminated A★★★'s sleeping face, and I couldn't help but stare. I was hoping that our unconscious nighttime bodily movements would culminate in a compromising position in the morning. But A★★★, always waking before me, eluded all fortuitous languor.

In the evenings, we would take a walk through the English garden nearby. At night, we would have dinner with some of A★★★'s friends before beginning our nocturnal wandering. We would walk from one club to another in the sharp cold of those December nights. The night before our departure, we completed a farewell tour. I still remember the amazing ambiance of the trashy dive we found ourselves in, a meeting point for homosexuals of all stripes, where A★★★ knew the owner, who was a former dancer. In the penumbra, further obscured by cigarette smoke and the movements of perspiring bodies packed one against the other, a barely visible transvestite burlesque show was unfolding. By contrast, the awkward stiffness of the Sans-Nom bored me and so we returned a bit earlier than usual to pack our bags. Worn out from visiting a number of museums that afternoon, I collapsed onto the bed, asleep, without taking the time to undress. From the depths of an intractable slumber, for a very brief moment, I vaguely perceived someone leaning over me, a vision of A★★★'s face near mine, the sensation of being tucked in. Then I plunged back, muttering, into an interrupted dream. Once again, I was stirred awake by the feeling of being touched and, in the uncertainty of shadows and the fog of sleep, I discerned A★★★ looking at me. Turning over, I groped in the darkness for A★★★'s body and threw myself against it before falling back to sleep.

I never alluded to what I had so indistinctly perceived in my sleep, and neither did A★★★. There were always inexplicable silences between us, a sort of prudishness or reserve that kept us from broaching certain intimate subjects. We kept the evidence hidden away, even avoiding the use of expressions that seemed improper, excessive, or bizarre. A★★★ would never show any immoderate affection, and I was constantly forcing myself not to criticize the escapades I witnessed. Once, only once, I was weak enough to reveal my jealousy, which had been gnawing away at me. In the same vein, A★★★ only once slipped in showing tenderness toward me, using words and gestures that we had never before allowed ourselves to use.

This single jealous episode took place in the dressing room of the Eden where, one night, I came upon A★★★ in the company of a man I had seen fairly often in the wings the previous week, whom I suspected to be A★★★'s latest lover. Normally I pretended not to give a damn about the goings-on of A★★★'s libido; the number and nature of A★★★'s escapades were none of my business. What right did I have to be jealous, since there was nothing between us other than platonic affection? But that night I could not bear to see this lugubrious cretin, in the seat that I habitually occupied, engaged with A★★★ in the sort of conversation I had thought was reserved for me alone. This substitution outraged me: the idea that in my absence someone could take my place, could be the object of identical attentions. I was willing to admit that I was not everything for A★★★, but I refused to accept that what I was, achieved through a hard-fought struggle, could be taken over by someone else, and apparently by *anyone at all*. The sole merit of the lover in question was his idiocy: his inane conversation was doubtless a nice break from the thornier discussions A★★★ and I typically had. A★★★ thought he had a beautiful face, entrancing eyes, and good fashion sense. I was shocked by A★★★'s poor taste, by the appreciation of such an individual: an Adonis from a centerfold with a stupidly handsome face.

I had judged him, a priori, as moronic, and I realized, triumph and despair mixing indissolubly, that it was true, indeed in every way. I was revolted by this pretty boy's attitude, by his dumbfounded acceptance and regurgitation of all conventional hogwash. With the aplomb bestowed on him by age and rank, Monsieur would uphold unconscionable vulgarities, which, moreover, he revered—a proselyte! When I arrived, the conversation was revolving around the countries of North Africa, which he had glimpsed during a recent trip to a resort. He passed briskly from the picturesque story of his trip to general commentary on the countries and the samples of the population that one could encounter in France, "in *our* country," as he articulated so well. I reveled in ridiculing a rival in front of A★★★ and put on a show of systematic perversity. The discussion quickly turned sour: when one realizes that one is being unreasonable, it is precisely then that one employs even more uncouth and violent arguments. The offspring of the 16th arrondissement do not like to be refuted, much less mocked; they never think it beneath them to resort to insults, no matter how low. I left, slamming the door behind me, not without having hurled out an extremely spiteful compliment on the quality and distinction of A★★★'s lover, whom I referred to with a far more offensive noun.

I was in a very bad mood when I arrived at the Apocryphe, and the music I selected was proof. I exuded my resentment through the loud-speakers, which calmed me down a bit. On the floor that night were some showbiz caryatids, those people that one sees on the covers of popular magazines. They did me the honor of a hello, expecting that I would carry out some of their desiderata: "Could you maybe play X's latest record…? He's here tonight, it would be an immmmense pleasure for him," or else: "When are you going to play some reggae?" It made me snicker that these dignitaries, flush with their new, modern-day power, solicited favors from the feeble authority conferred on me by my position behind the turntables. What an *enormous* privilege it was in their eyes that they should notice me! In granting me the favor of acknowledging my presence, of pouring onto me a miniscule portion of the celebrity they oozed and tried to pawn off as glory, they tried cheaply to coax my kindness. I made them feel the vanity of their approach, and unless they were willing to own up to the humiliation of failure, they had no choice but to laugh at my sneering. And that night in particular they were made to feel the grace of my cynicism, the bursts of my impertinent irony.

Common mortals have other ways of expressing their desires. A club does not get filled every night with only the chic clientele. Because there are a paltry number of remarkable characters—and they are remarkable only because their number is paltry—a mass of individuals of lower distinction are allowed into this sanctuary, a privilege through which they are made to feel honored. They would come to the Apocryphe, attracted by the club's reputation (they don't accept just *anybody*—you, me, any old person), hoping to rub shoulders with some celebrities.

That night I realized something: they pronounce their desiderata, demanding (without really caring) some record, in order to prove that they have a right to be in this milieu where the arbitrary reigns. It's their sole ontological proof, their sole cogito, their foundation and justification.

I want, therefore I am; I need, I breathe. I spend money, they must grant my desire, considering my demands in light of the value that I offer. I pay to exist; the tribute, delivered in kind or in cash, buys the recognition of my right.

My strategy was to inspire incertitude; I derived pleasure in imbuing these souls with doubt by not playing into their pathetic ruses. *Che vuoi?* I was leading them to the brink of an essential anxiety. My reply was always "maybe." It was a dangerous game that exposed me to the disapproval, disrespect, or insidious resentment of the people to whom I denied the assurance of being a subject. Each night I would have to confront this great panic of individual desires that were in reality desires for individuation, for furious revindication. Sometimes I would try—utterly in vain but with a perverse pleasure—to make them understand that the sum of individual desires does not add up to the happiness of all. That when it comes to the music in a club the law of the majority is ineffectual; that neither democracy nor aristocracy, nor even oligarchy, is a possible regime for a coherent musical set. I would argue that a good DJ is one who, rather than simply responding to repetitive wishes that are consciously formulaic and elementary (such and such a record, such and such a song), subconsciously manages to fulfill an unknown desire by creating a unity out of something superior to adding up so many records, so many requests. To appease is not the same as to fulfill.

Each night I made such observations that I would occasionally articulate to myself when pedantic disquisition and contempt started to mutually reinforce each other. I had come to the end of this chapter of my *De natura rerum noctis* dedicated to the essence of the position of the DJ when I noticed A★★★ standing near the bar, no longer accompanied by that new moronic lover, being served a glass of champagne by the barman.

It was late, the Eden had already been closed for some time, and

I worried that A★★★'s arrival at the Apocryphe after our altercation meant trouble. I didn't know if I was supposed to leave my booth and go meet A★★★ or if I was supposed to wait for A★★★ to approach me. Fortunately, we both had the same reflex, and met halfway between the bar and the booth. There was no visible trace of what had happened a few hours before. A★★★ was drunk, which almost never happened, and from within that drunkenness asked me to dance. People didn't dance as a couple anymore in those days except during retro sequences when the DJ would revive old dance forms such as the bop, tango, or waltz. And that was absolutely what A★★★ desired: a waltz, nothing less. I was enticed by this extravagance, and besides, why not? At this late hour, only a small number of people remained on the floor. A waltz would serve as a charming exit, and, irresistibly outmoded, could assume the parodic allure that excuses all improprieties. So from the bottom of the crate I took out an LP of Viennese waltzes that I cued with no transition, following some non-descript funk track. Abandoning the turntables, and without any snarky retort this time, I went to dance this waltz.

A★★★, though drunk, was dancing divinely. A classic routine demonstrates one's sensibility just as much as the unruly improvisations of today's dance steps. While dancing these waltzes—for we danced many in succession—I had the impression that never until this day had I reveled in such a carefree lightness of being. There was no longer anybody but us on the dance floor; no doubt our perfect execution of the steps had intimidated all the amateurs. A★★★ had a naïve and clichéd fondness for the antiquated world of the aristocracy, an admiration for the bygone, the retro, the image of luxury that Hollywood associates with times past.

A★★★'s drunkenness, at once dissipated and concentrated by the dance, kept us moving. When the Apocryphe closed, we hurried to the Kormoran. Ruggero had a bottle of whiskey brought to my table that he insisted on offering me for the New Year, and as a thank you for the cigars I had brought him back from Germany. And so I too started to drink. A★★★ and I talked for a long time about everything under the sun. We were drunk, A★★★ more so than me. There was a warmth, a hint of complicity between us, which soothed the constant tension of our unfinished business. And this happy understanding, permitted by our drunkenness, was further reinforced by the illusory intensity of perception brought on by the alcohol. Leaning toward me and speaking with more abandon than usual, A★★★ suddenly murmured the following question: "And if we make love, will you still love me after?" Abruptly, I caught a glimpse of what I had given up hoping for, without ever having written it off. It was finally being offered to me, in a whisper and under the extraordinary guise of a fiction, all that we had envisioned and elaborated, that which ultimately gave meaning to all of our stratagems. A★★★ repeated the query, making it sound like a supplication. I leaned toward A★★★, not knowing how to respond to the anxiety I sensed in the question.

My only answer was to wrest A★★★ from the chair and to take us out of this place. Once outside and without having discussed it at all, we hailed a taxi and A★★★ told the driver the address. Without saying a word, we took the elevator. The fear that I had forgotten suddenly returned and took me by the heart, the fear of flesh that accompanies those first adolescent excitements, an anxiety we attempt to combat too quickly with cynicism. I thought I was going to faint, standing there at last on the threshold of what I had so passionately desired.

I staggered as A★★★ moved to kiss me; I didn't know what to do except let it happen. The temporal order of events, even the simple spatial points of reference, all disappeared without my realizing it; everything is blurred in my memory. I have in my mouth, still, the taste of skin, of the sweat on that skin; against my hands, the tactile impression of skin and the shape of that flesh. In a sprawling obscurity—either I closed my eyes or my gaze was struck with a temporary blindness—some vaguely outlined visions, and, in my ear, the echo of soft rustlings, of words barely articulated.

I don't know how to recount precisely what happened, or how to describe or even attest to what I did, what was done to me. And the effect of the alcohol has nothing to do with this eradication; it's impossible to recapture the feeling of abandon through words. Crotches crossed and sexes mixed, I no longer knew how to distinguish anything. In this confusion we slept.

When I awoke from the incredible sleep that follows the appeasement of the flesh, I saw A★★★, watching me and smoking a cigarette. The memories I have of my life at that time are all of this order. Dissolved are the restless nights, the clammy visions of crowds of bodies mangled and shredded by the spurts of light that cut through shadow. Crystallized at the bottom of my memory remains the recollection of these sleeps and these wakings where one floats between the resurgence of desire and the memory of its satisfaction.

Never until then had I longed to see A★★★ dance on stage. When A★★★ danced in the Apocryphe, I didn't have to share the pleasure I took in watching: I was allowed to imagine that the dance was dedicated entirely to me, without the crowd being there to prove me wrong. Watching this body moving uninhibited, this body that wasn't mine in any way, I reveled in the uniqueness and the exclusivity of my gaze.

However, not long after that first night, I decided to go and watch the show put on at the Eden. From my place in the audience, I watched A★★★ perform one of the club's best numbers. I can only describe it as a syncopated progression of movements, the ecstatic miming of a song written in English entitled—I learned later—"Sphinx." I was struck by the lyrics, at least by the ones I could grasp in the moment. I came back to this song so many times, keeping it as an emblem, the enigmatic prophecy of all that ever came to pass between A★★★ and me. I was struck that night by certain lines, which I deciphered or guessed from watching their silent pronunciation on A★★★'s lips. Erratic blocks of words, fragments that resounded in me even more violently because they were incomplete, that I grasped only insofar as they seemed to articulate something of my relationship to this strange figure I had only recently succeeded in conquering.

Later I translated the exact words of the song and watched as their meaning, which I had imperfectly intuited that night, unfolded. I transcribe the essential lines here:

> *I can't stand the pain*
> *and I keep looking for all the faces I had*
> *before the world began.*
> *I've only known desire and my poor soul will burn*
> *into eternal fire.*
> *And I can't even cry,*
> *a sphinx can never cry.*
> *I wish that I could be*
> *a silent sphinx eternally.*
> *I don't want any past*
> *only want things which cannot last.*
> *Phony words of love*
> *or painful truth, I've heard it all before.*
> *A conversation piece,*
> *a woman or a priest, it's all a point of view.*

The vision comes back to me instantly: A★★★ crossing the stage in the feline roving of the choreography, embodying an enigmatic, silent figure twisting to the extreme limit of dislocation in miraculous movements that were syncopated but not staccato. Even as this body fades away, a spectral figure remains, immobile; the stage is populated with incarnations, sudden gestures, hieratic poses set in a relentless progression. There was something cat-like or divine in this body that, moved by some sly, sensual pleasure, was embodying in nonchalant strides a languid damnation, an immemorial fatality made into movement.

When I entered the dressing room, I found A★★★ immobile as if in prayer or confession, legs bent, forearms fixed on a high barstool supporting A★★★'s entire body weight. Hands dangling, wrists slack, gaze abandoned and lost in the emptiness, then focusing on me as I entered and following me to where I sat down opposite. It was like the disdainful pose of the sphinx (or the image I had of it then), the same sharp aesthetic. I thought this to myself and, laughing, affectionately let slip, "my sphinx"—as if I had said "my love." We remained face-to-face, our bodies as if petrified. A terror silted up in my throat; the desire I had felt welling up in me at the sight of those distant movements on the stage had been suspended. I could do nothing but adore. Those eyes, so black, fixed on me, subjected me to an unbearable torture.

The following winter we planned a trip to New York to visit A★★★'s family, including A★★★'s mother, uncles, aunts, and cousins. We thought of it as a break, an interpolated parenthesis in the delirious lifestyle caused by our jobs. We wanted a rest from the excitement—and the resulting comedown—of our nights of partying, to flee the invasive rumble of the social scene. We also wanted to repair the damage done by A★★★'s inability to remain faithful to me, by those passing flings that always led to remorse and then a sudden resurgence of desire and a whirlwind week of all kinds of debaucheries. We were hoping that through a month of intimacy, of living free from constraint, we could erase the hurts that a year of voracious and nocturnal passion had inflicted on us.

We left right at the beginning of January, not long after the New Year. The day we arrived we visited A★★★'s mother, whom I was meeting for the first time. She was living alone in a studio, on the twelfth floor of a building on Second Avenue. Behind her apparent reserve upon their reunion, which contrasted starkly with the effusive demonstration of affection deployed by A★★★, I perceived the joy, or rather the painful relief, brought on by this homecoming. The insidious pain inflicted on her by A★★★'s long absence seeped through her happiness. I sensed the misery, the despair caused by the distance from the sole person she loved. She wouldn't even allow herself to show this sadness, so deep was the wound. She considered me attentively without asking any questions and, it seemed, accepted me without need for discussion. I was there with A★★★, who seemed to be attached to me and to whom I seemed to be attached. What did she suspect our relationship to be? What did she think of it? I never knew. All I learned, which I heard through A★★★, was that she appreciated my attentiveness and my lack of histrionics. Of all the people she had had the occasion to see in A★★★'s company, it was for me, apparently, that she had the most esteem. She was astonished by how young I was (ten years younger than A★★★). She thought it was a good omen that I wasn't particularly extroverted. I think she feared for A★★★, not knowing anything about her child's life, and what she imagined or heard of it did not reassure her in the least. And, though she never regarded A★★★ with disapproval, she did not manage to conceal her anxiety. She was as apprehensive of meeting me as she was excited: she was no doubt dreading that she would not care for me as much as A★★★ was counting on it.

We stayed in a hotel for three nights, waiting for one of my former fellow university students to hand over his apartment in the city, which we would stay in during his upcoming absence. Our room, on the 25th floor of a modern building, opened onto East 42nd Street. We had agreed to spend our first nights in luxury: the room was big, the bathroom adorned with marble, and the bed immense. Despite the long trip and despite being awake for more than 24 hours, we weren't tired at all, nor did we want to sleep. Through the taxi window, I had avidly observed all that passed before my eyes: the graffiti on the palisades and walls; the waves of oversized cars; the baroque decay of certain neighborhoods; the diversity of the people walking on the sidewalks. I felt intoxicated; the dreams I had suppressed in my state of prolonged wakefulness were turning everything I saw into visions: eyes open, I was dreaming this newly discovered city. The almost electric atmosphere of this place, completely new to me, was as exciting for me as it was for A★★★, whose childhood and adolescence had been lived out in this familiar setting. For the first time, we could feel like a couple; in this restless, teeming city we were experiencing an ineffable, exalting feeling of intimacy and togetherness. The city before our eyes and under our feet united us through its simple strangeness or familiarity. I was trying to decipher the traces of A★★★'s past life, and for A★★★ this trip served as a type of secret confession.

Turning away from the window where I had been contemplating the night sky and the horizon of lights, I did a little dance toward the bed. A★★★ came out of the shower, wearing only a towel. I coaxed A★★★ onto the bed, and then held my new prisoner captive between my arms and legs. As we rolled around, a juvenile excitement seized me, the desire to play, to roughhouse, to run out of breath doing something frivolous. I couldn't remember having had such a desire for a long time; I had forgotten that state of mind, lost since childhood, and it returned to me suddenly in a hotel room smack in the middle of New York. I whispered inconsequential words in A★★★'s ear, who could do nothing but laugh. My body was immense; it could have embraced all of America. The blood in my arteries, the air in my lungs, the ideas in my head all shared the same lightness. I horsed around with A★★★ like I had never dared to do before, allowing myself the liberties and improprieties that formerly I had thought of as obscene, but which now seemed innocently naïve. When asked what I was doing, I replied that I had finished my homework and certainly had the right to play with my toys before my afternoon snack.

When we finally found ourselves side by side, smoking the inevitable cigarette, I said to A★★★, after a moment of silence and reflection, that it felt as if we had never, before this day, truly made love. For an entire year we had only endeavored to reach a very crude form of ecstasy. After the subtle sensuality we had just shared, all the other times seemed like a laborious peccadillo. I concluded that making love without laughing was as bad as gifting a book written in a language the recipient does not know. The obscurity of my metaphor perplexed A★★★; already my more serious side was feeling neglected. I leapt out of bed and proposed we go for a walk.

It was one in the morning, the air was cold but not freezing. We walked up Fifth Avenue. When we reached the edge of Central Park, there was silence: it had begun to snow. Horse-drawn carriages were still stationed before the Plaza. Our eyes were shining; I wondered whether A★★★'s body and heart felt as light as mine did. A★★★ was humming a song that I often put on at the Apocryphe toward the end of the night: "La Ville Inconnue." I laced our arms together and began to sing along. Our two breaths condensed upon contact with the cold air and formed a cloud, as if the song was materializing before us.

By the time we got back to the hotel, the sidewalks were covered with a fine layer of snow violated only by our footprints. We lay down in the immense bed, shoulder-to-shoulder right in the middle, leaving a large white border on each side.

· · · · · · · · · · · · · · · · ·

I know essentially nothing of white, Anglo-Saxon, Puritan America. My own America is of black origins—the music, the voices, the food. There's a term for that in the black community: soul. Soul music, soul food. The nourishment of the soul?

Accompanying A★★★ to family reunions and meals during the season's festivities, I found myself lost in the heart of a neighborhood where white people rarely ventured—some remote suburb of Long Island or New Jersey. For two days the women had been preparing a Southern-style meal, paying tribute to the family's roots.

I hardly know the names of these dishes, let alone how they're prepared.

I lived among this family only the length of brief visits and, from one year to the next, I ate these dishes over and over again, without ever seeking to educate myself about them. I didn't feel the need. It sufficed simply to be there, as if I had always belonged to their world. Others in my place would probably have tried to play the explorer and make curious inquiries, as an anthropologist or a traveler greedy to understand how or why. But what did I care? I felt at home there, so much did they make me feel like a part of their family, effortlessly forgetting our differences in race, color, culture, class—everything that one might cite as possible traits of alterity. It was as if the language they were speaking and the food they were cooking had always been familiar to me.

And the old black mommas laughed with delight to see that I had such an appetite. A★★★, who was used to seeing me bored or indifferent when faced with earthly sustenance, was astonished and overjoyed. I was forgetting to repine, I was finally tasting life, savoring each bite without the table-talk that, in Europe generally, and in France particularly, constitutes the essential component of meals.

Even now, the taste of sweet potato melts into the taste of iced tea in my mouth. Is there anything more vertiginous than gustative reminiscence? For it upends completely the conventional workings of memory. When I recall this meal, something appears without being summoned, something that does not serve as a witness to anything, that does not help me to follow the thread of my memory. But this something returns—not under the guise of a phantom, of an immaterial representation of an object now vanished, of a perception swallowed up and designated to a bygone past, coming from the imagination to reincarnate itself feebly in the present. Instead, it crystallizes, taking on an intense, fugitive form, a carnal presence—the rebirth of a sensation whose former source has long ago disappeared. A vivid hallucination, a tangible reliving that invades the mouth and spreads down the back of the throat, taking on body, flesh, and warmth: the flavor itself, still intact, of this long-gone nourishment.

Then the taste that surfaced on my tongue is erased, mutated in the caress of this persistent flavor that I feel melt and travel to the bottom of my throat. Even as the pure gustatory reminiscence that surged up in me at the evocation of tea and sweet potatoes fades and dissolves, the sensation of gooiness comes back to me: those melting granules that coat the epithelium as far back as the glottis in a soft, thick veil, as would honey. I silently revel in this sweetness descending in me, fearing that with words I might tear the surface of this veil, both fragile and protective, like a second skin.

My English still bears the stigmata from the time spent among an almost exclusively black community. Imperceptibly, the expressions and characteristic improprieties of their speech slipped into the tissue of the academic English I had been taught in high school. The language I speak is a monstrous hybrid, mingling Oxford and Harlem, Byron and gospel. To the point of caricature, I pronounce these African American utterances with a *rather British* accent, and sometimes swallow up to half of the syllables of a too perfectly constructed sentence.

· · · · · · · · · · · · · · · · ·

I begged A★★★, who was strongly repelled by the idea, to take me on a walk through Harlem. My wish was finally granted after several entreaties. One afternoon, we went up the main avenue of Harlem on foot, from Central Park up to 125th Street. I exalted in the view of these neighborhoods whose ruin and incredible devastation reminded me, in places, of Berlin: the vestiges of a past splendor, as if swept away by a brutal disaster. People congregated in doorways, busy conducting transactions, and watched us pass out of the corner of their eyes, indifferent. In a run-down building with neither doors nor windows and open to gusts of winter wind, vagrants had lit a brazier to heat their hands over the flames. The snow shoveled into heaps on the sidewalks was turning into ice now that the sun had begun to sink behind the towers of lower Manhattan. We walked slowly; after 110th Street we no longer saw a single white person, nor even a Puerto Rican. Like all who have left Harlem, it repulsed A*** to be back, even temporarily, so disconcerting was the spectacle of abandon and misery plastered on the fronts of buildings. The day was dimming. The more we walked into the heart of this city, the heavier and more pressing was the feeling of affliction. Shadow was eroding the facades, riddled with the holes of what were once windows. Desolation was spread uniformly over this inordinate expanse; the excessive degradation would have been heartrending even for those who tend to savor macabre spectacles. Harlem projected the muffled but poignant impression of the end of the world. This vision haunted me for a long time. I felt as though there, amidst all the abandonment, I had abandoned something of myself, snatched away without my realizing it in the moment and subsequently forever out of reach. I wasn't able to close the wound that had been opened by this cleaving of my own flesh.

The effect of this sundering has never left me; sometimes I am forced to relive certain moments all over again, vivid and uncorrupted, when, digressing at random, my thoughts bring old memories back to me. An anxiety wells up and distills in me, the feeling of having lost, of having let this setting swallow up, a fragment of my substance that I can't place or describe, but whose absence makes itself felt throughout my body, invading and voiding it insidiously. A bitter cold, an abyss full of wind cuts through me, the same wind that cut through me as I walked through the streets of Harlem all those years ago. Harlem's devastation now resides in me, my body haunted by the soul of this spectral city. It's a dead body that I carry, lodged in the depths of my own, which is at the brink of death as a result. And Harlem retains something of me, too; I still have visions of this loss. I am forced to remember this place's existence because of this theft, its resurgence in my memory, the sorrow I feel but cannot define; it doesn't want to leave me, it refuses to close the door on its misery, instead poisoning the vague wave of my thoughts, invading me, stripping me, emptying me of all that is not it, taking possession of my body, staking itself and taking refuge, overwhelming the physical limits of time and distance, absorbing me into itself, turning my body into that city, that abandonment, that devastation.

When we returned from America, I resumed my position behind the turntables at the Apocryphe, but only on Thursdays, Fridays, and Saturdays—the nights with the biggest crowds. I had resolved to resume my studies and to devote my four days off per week to analyzing metaphysical texts in order to write an essay on the apophatic tradition.

For too long I had neglected a regular intellectual practice because it had been incompatible with the new mind-numbing nocturnal life to which I had made myself prisoner. I became aware of these constraints and of their consequences once I had had a vacation from them, a pause that suspended the chain of overindulgent nights. It made me realize the bleak inanity of the time I had lost squandering my life in the night, devoting myself exclusively to venal pleasures.

The Eden had closed—momentarily, so they said—and A***, with neither work nor guaranteed income, moved in with me. Living together seemed only natural following a month of vacation without any drama, and the vastness of my apartment spared us from sharing any awkward propinquity.

The airy, sweet closeness was not, however, without tension, brought on by the radical difference in our lifestyles. All day we stayed in the house, barely leaving; but while I withdrew to my study to read in peace, A*** would spend most days in front of the television screen watching shows and films, despite my attempts to suggest a less passive pastime.

No book or work of art was enticing enough to evoke curiosity. A★★★'s sole activity was a daily exercise routine to maintain good physical form and bodily suppleness. At the end of each week, we would have dinner together at a restaurant before heading to the Apocryphe, or, when A★★★ felt the desire (more and more frequently) to meet up with some friends, we would separate at the door of the club, where I would carry out my night's work.

In April I took a three-month vacation, which we spent visiting some cities in Europe before continuing on to New York. Venice, Florence, Rome, Munich, Heidelberg, Berlin, Amsterdam, and London: we made a tour of these cities over the course of May and June without spending more than a week in any of them. In the space of a few days, I would visit the museums that I knew had some paintings (by Mantegna in particular) or collections I was hoping to see. I also visited a few universities where I had friends who introduced me to the professors there who might be interested in my research. They were all very welcoming and encouraged me to pursue my studies.

A★★★ followed me begrudgingly into the museums in Italy, preferring to enjoy the sea and to tan through long—and, in my opinion, inhuman—sessions. A★★★ found the cities of the North disappointing and boring, devoid of charm as picturesque as that of the Alps. In Berlin, as in London, we went to the opera as well as to some classical concerts, which for A★★★ were mere social occasions, failing to incite any profound interest. The only things that provided A★★★ with an unfeigned pleasure were walks through the streets, from café to café, from fashion boutique to jeweler's.

New York was less boring, because it was a familiar city where A★★★ could demonstrate superiority over me. We experienced an extraordinary resurgence of our passion; the city's power and excitement infiltrated us just as it had during our first visit. It was summer, and the heat, not too excessive, made for pleasant walks through the streets. The nights, singularly electric, lured us out. The clubs and bars were crowded with vacationing students who had come to New York to revel in the monstrous buzz of the artistic and cultural scene.

Basking in a renewal of passion for the world, for life, and for our love, we shared secrets, words, and caresses profusely, allowing ourselves to forget all our past hurts and to believe for a moment in an idyll whose state of grace lingered even after we had left its source, that city.

The Eden reopened in September with a brand new show on the billing. A★★★ was asked to join the new troupe. The rehearsals took up the end of August, with six hours of work a day and up to ten hours in the days preceding the premiere.

We rarely saw each other. During the day, I stayed in to work in my study without going out, while A★★★, with renewed professional rigor, met the artistic and physical demands of preparation. In the evening, we would eat dinner together and then go to bed very early. The nights when I was working, A★★★, who had stopped going out, stayed at the apartment. Returning at daybreak, I would go to sleep in the bed that A★★★ would soon be vacating.

I don't know whether it was A★★★'s absence or a kind of unhinging, a solitude induced by the disjunction in our lifestyles, that was producing this effect, but clubs were now inspiring only a growing boredom in me, dangerously close to contempt. I was about to turn twenty-three, and for the three years the night crowd had passed before my eyes, I had seen reputations be made and dismantled. I had seen temporary passions transport places and individuals to the apex, and then, burning what they had once adored, those notorious night owls who make up the club scene would abandon them for no apparent reason for other idols destined for a glory just as brief.

It was a never-ending cycle: a new club would open with flashier décor than ever and resounding, luminous sound equipment more over the top and expensive that anything we had seen before. Always bigger, better, louder, more exclusive and more chichi: the propensity to outdo others governed the cycles of this sparkling microcosm. But behind the circus I discerned only a dreadful repetition; the same shady characters would dominate this market where the figureheads, straw men, and wax mannequins were waltzing to an infernal rhythm. For ages, some thirty individuals, usually vulgar and with unconvincing respectability, would hide behind the scenes and open, close, and resell the clubs, all conceived on the same model. The machine was running on empty, racing, turning out a fortune without producing an iota of delight: no one enjoyed themselves in the least in these clubs, and I started to doubt whether anyone ever had.

Money, reigning despotically, was reducing these places to nothing more than interchangeable settings for dreary prostitution and, to make up for this disgrace, they were rotten with snobbery. The only people seen there, noisily upstaging everyone else, were the *nouveau riche* and the horde of thieves that money draws: dealers, prostitutes, gigolos, and crooks of all calibers. For the sake of appearance or photo opportunities, the crowd was sprinkled with a few celebrities, people who were recognized and idolized.

I could no longer bear the assault of this ambient vulgarity. Behind the simulacrum of festivity and opulence, I witnessed the most sordid trafficking and the seediest machinations, sheepishly disguised. The four months I stayed on in Paris were a calvary for me: the obligatory visits to this cloacum were nauseating. I was being drained by my academic essay whose subject was as far as possible from what I confronted on a daily basis. And finally, I was suffering from the distance I felt growing between A★★★ and me. We continued to live together, yet we scarcely spent time together.

Without realizing it, I started longing for my detour via the Eden, those rendezvous from the first days of our relationship, the route that I took every night to the Apocryphe. Disgust at the milieu we now took no pleasure in visiting was gradually surfacing, combining destructively with the loss of substance in our relationship.

We had sealed within ourselves all the dissatisfaction, resentment, and suffering our surroundings had generated. Side by side, we were incubating our grievances. Our relationship suffered profoundly for it: we gave free reign to our mood swings without any creative effort to break through the distance establishing itself between us. A terrible wound opened from all that was eating away at us.

Crisis erupted upon our return from a week spent in New York for the New Year, when we fell once again into the hell we had unknowingly emerged from for a moment. Its abrupt, stifling horror filled us with distress, the same distress walling us in through the dissolution of our love, through a distance that was making us practically strangers to each other. All that the outside inflicted on us resulted in a growing tension, which we never let dissolve in a moribund agreement.

One evening, we turned on each other in the dressing room of the Eden where A★★★ was getting ready to go on stage. I haphazardly reproached A★★★ for being cold and uncaring, for being shamefully narcissistic, too. I was reproached in turn for never having asked myself what I really wanted our relationship to be, for never allowing it to run smoothly by fault of never having considered, or taken into account, anything other than an image, other than my singular, and therefore false, vision of A★★★, with which I had been complacent.

We reached a point of extreme irritation, throwing in each other's face absolutely anything that came to mind. I demanded to know what was wanted of me, what need I had to satisfy. We only cut ourselves off when a stagehand entered with A★★★'s costume. Leaving the dressing room, A★★★, from the door, turned back and hurled this question at me without waiting for a response: "How do you see me, anyway?"

After A★★★ left, I lingered in the dressing room's usual disorder. My gaze fell upon a large mirror opposite the door, which had slammed shut after the question. I stared at the door's reflection. A response came to my lips, which I murmured pensively in the silence: "I see you in a mirror."

I was waiting for the show to finish so I could deliver that reply—a reply that gave me an odd satisfaction. It was not quite a reply, in fact: it was an enigma, an obscure sentence, a fragment of an aphorism in the tone of an apocalyptic prophesy. I turned it over and over in my mind, on my lips, and before my eyes without diminishing its charm or unveiling its meaning.

An unexpected uproar pulled me from my lethargic, mesmerized meditation. The show must have been coming to a close, but the rumble that usually accompanied the finale had never taken on such proportions. I got up from the couch and started toward the hallway. On the threshold, I paused for a moment and glanced over my shoulder to glimpse my reflection in the mirror.

I tried to see from the wings what was causing all this commotion. On the stage, at the bottom of the large staircase at the back, was a confused cluster of bodies, some of them almost naked, others in work overalls or in evening wear. Arms, heads, and ostrich feathers were sprouting out of the crowd. Rumbles and indistinct murmurs traveled through the chaotic hall. A firefighter, jostling me, raced onto the stage; the rest of the troupe rushed from the dressing rooms, carrying me in its throng, packing me into the mass. In order to reassure the audience, a stage manager grabbed a microphone to announce that the show had been momentarily interrupted, and to beseech all those who had no business being on the stage please to clear away. Ebbing, the circle moved aside and, in the interstice between a heap of feathers and the imposing stature of a stagehand, with heartrending terror I saw A***'s body, which I recognized even before having truly discerned it, sprawled and immobile on the ground, with two men trying to place it on a stretcher.

While everyone else evacuated the stage, I approached and followed the stretcher into the wings. They brought the body to the dressing room where a doctor, summoned for the emergency, came bursting in shortly after. I stood next to the lifeless body that in my terror I didn't dare touch—I knew already, obscurely, that a gruesome misfortune I was afraid to name had taken place. Next entered a small group of dancers who came upon hearing the news. The doctor, leaning over the body, straightened up. Seeing that I was watching him, he pronounced his conclusion volubly. Apparently, a break in the cervical spine had provoked an instant and probably painless death.

A murmur rose from the back of the room; the doctor was already on his way out. Some of the dancers, still half-naked, approached the body. They had seen A*** trip, fall headfirst, and violently hurtle down the entire flight of stairs, helpless to resist or direct the fall. At the foot of the stairs, the dislocated body, following a scream that had sprung forth from every mouth, had remained still in the silence of death that preceded the general tumult.

The show was suspended only briefly. They replaced A*** off the cuff with another member of the troupe. The presenter reassured the spectators of the fate of the victim of this regrettable accident, and they redid the finale (which A***'s fall had interrupted) in its entirety. Mourning isn't much suited to venal celebrations. The show was performed two times each night for successive batches of clients, and the second performance of that night went on as usual, quite naturally and without mishap.

I remained in the dressing room with A★★★'s body, and the director came to convey his condolences to me and to assure me that he would take care of all the formalities and cover the costs until the insurance money came through. He left, and I found myself again head to head with the cadaver still spread upon the stretcher that had served to transport it, which the two stagehands had set up on a trestle in the middle of the room.

For three hours I stood before this vision of a beloved body I knew to be dead, without the fact resounding in me sufficiently to shift my sentiment or my gaze. To my right, in the mirror on top of the vanity table, was the body's reflection. From my view, due to a frightening effect of perspective, the body's image was foreshortened, from the soles of the feet in the foreground up to the head, which was lost in the distance in a virtual space that swallowed up my gaze, stumbling up against the base of the chin, boring into the gaps of the nostrils, and fading along the line of the eyebrows beyond which the forehead faded away. It was as if this sprawled body in the mirror was looming over my gaze.

A halo of lamps, the sole source of light, framed the mirror and bathed the painting taking shape there in a pale shadow; the reflection was melting A★★★'s body and my face at its side into one single lividity.

III

From then on I didn't get out of bed until dusk; in the night, my infernal refuge, I indulged in roving fantasies.

A★★★'s presence was stolen from me by images. While we were together, I was jealous of all that had engrossed A★★★. I hated the television, detested those frivolous parties and their cortèges of ostentatious, superficial people. All the time stolen from me by those hours spent shopping, at the jeweler's, the hairdresser's, all of that dissipated time. Although, to be fair: some moments of pure pomp had fascinated me as well, the times I watched A★★★'s body mutate into an image. What price did I pay for them, in suffering? When we lived together, I always interrupted my eternal, languishing reverie to spy on the slow ceremony of applying makeup in the bathroom—the brushstrokes that highlighted the cheekbones, the sharp line of the pencil, the superimposition of different colors on the eyelids to intensify the socket. But I would lose myself in the distance of the gaze, closing myself off in mere vision. Little by little, my gaze, isolated in the mirror—a living enclave—became petrified in the glass facade formed around that face.

Everything stole A★★★'s presence from me: the infinitely expanding circle of high society friends, A★★★ playing the role of social butterfly no matter where we went. I salvage crumbs of A★★★'s presence, captured fragments snatched from the brutal dissipation of that life. From this debris, I recreated an entirely other life, the one I would have liked to live in A★★★'s company if it had not been for the seduction of anything and everything that sparkled. The time we spent together was dedicated to this imaginary, deflected, and diverted reconstruction of every act, gesture, and word, with the secret intention of thus being able to appropriate and incorporate A★★★. The strange sensation of never being able to grasp or embrace A★★★ except in the painting I was reconstructing from those idealized fragments of real life. The strange temptation to recreate a life in which I had felt only barely included: it seemed as though none of A★★★'s words or gestures had been for me. I was the shadow of a body that ignored me; I was also the source of light that produced that shadow. All that came back to me was a projection of myself. A★★★ was merely a parasite interposed between my consciousness and my unfailing tendency to diffract the real.

The one I loved I saw as dead, had to imagine as dead, had to think of in the past tense in order to bring about my own satisfaction from this living cadaver, a fulfillment that the real being had unconsciously refused me, for I was incapable of enjoying reality. I knew this was a morbid exercise, and had often been afraid that A★★★ would notice the crumbling happening underground; I was mining a life. How could I have only derived pleasure from my vision of A★★★ by imagining that all I saw already belonged to death? How could I have seen A★★★'s death as a side effect of my happiness in our life together? Before, I was mourning the present; today I mourn a past that was never present. I mourn a funereal existence, devoted to the vampirization of the flesh that made me feel an agonizing impotence because I was not able to take possession of it except through murder and mummification. Like a parasite, I fed on the images that stole A★★★'s presence from me, images that, in this henceforth deserted world, are incapable of restoring to me even one iota of A★★★'s presence.

· · · · · · · · · · · · · · · · ·

All those who captivated me thereafter always irremediably betrayed or disenchanted me. The spark they held in my eyes would pass too quickly, consumed, vanished, leaving me as nothing but a heap of dismal flesh, enlivened by a furious access of pettiness or hysteria.

I appear to myself in the guise of the hero of that 1950s novel entitled, for reasons I no longer remember, *La Chute*. A pure soul, all grandeur in a heroic mask, suffering and cheaply acting out the sublime in a chaotic confusion of good intentions and pious lucidities. However, something of my true self remained: the intimate sensation I derived from these passions, soon shattered by the aftertaste of falling out of love.

The strange sensation of always feeling as if I were at the dreadful edge of some imminent break…This sentiment is the very foundation of all that is intractable in me: a sort of inebriation, bitter from drawn-out solitude, the inevitable tendency toward a final disenchantment with all idylls. And I can't explain why, or how. I've never expected much from those I love. I would have given all, conceded all, pardoned all the wandering of anyone who accorded me the space and time for my discreet tenderness. So much did I fear smothering those I cherished that I never made a fuss, which was doubtless the reason for my repeated falls and defeats. I carry my silence—this constant withdrawal into a suffering that I thought of perhaps mistakenly as immoderate and obscene—as a cross that has never promised any redemption, a calvary without deliverance, an involuntary sacrifice made in vain.

Was I incorrigible to always lock away my grievances, wishing my partner would do the same? In silence I endured all transgressions, from the most trivial to the most serious (and my partner never understood which were the most serious for me, accumulating them innocently and obviously, but hiding those betrayals that didn't matter to me at all:

this burglary of the truth, more than the fault concealed, was what made me suffer). And because of my attention to decorum and my fear of a vulgar lover's tiff, I never dared to counter this extreme violence with anything of the same order. I deployed an irony that harmed only me, opening more fully the wound it was attempting to bandage.

My obsessive fear of this imminent fall was always hovering over me. How often did I imagine myself gripped with terror, collapsing, tumbling from the height of the relative safety of whatever promontory I had been occupying? A fall brought about by a purely internal and continually foreseen rending, imminently suspended on a final thread that never broke but which, taut and twisted unbearably, never ceased to tremble. The agonizing tension of always being about to crack without ever feeling the relief of chaos—for I denied myself even the obscene plenitude of annihilation.

In those moments when it seemed the dreaded, desired fall was drawing close, I don't know if I fled. At the least I retreated from its too-pressing arrival, as far as possible from whatever was seeming to provoke it. Somehow, I escaped. Probably through desertion, an abdication that threw me back into its core: an indissoluble knot of lonely meditation and troubled absence (I often imaged asceticism as being trapped inside a bedroom in a foreign town: New York, somewhere relatively high up, a decaying skyscraper in a pool of ruins, shaken from its foundations by the rhythm of African American voices: a syncopated version of Stendhal syndrome). By distancing myself from the world, I was squandering my destiny: such was the malediction of recognizing the world's infamy but not allowing myself to spit in its face.

The passion of my inner secret cohabited violently with the constant exhibitionism demanded of a social life, and I was unable to escape from it, to defend myself against it, or to decline its imperative invitation.

My mind was too supervised and civilized for this world that had become savage, imprinted with *savoir-vivre*, with a restraint that has become outdated but that remains the sole condition of civility. A drama was playing out and I was the battlefield. Who has resisted the temptation, the contempt evoked by this old Europe recalling the nostalgic charm of naphthalene? With a pure soul and the face of a martyr, I jeered at it, and yet I wasn't composed of anything better. The whole dialectic of Reason, the confused potage of the True, the Good, and the Beautiful was suddenly overthrown, tossed into the impetuous cloacum of a world that breaks through old barriers and overflows its first cradle, twisting and restless with tumults and tremblings provoked by these unseen, submarine restraints.

Moments, fragments come back to me. One morning at the Kormoran, the sight of A★★★ brought tears to my eyes: I was imagining this body, lost, dead, vanished. I used to love watching it move, hips and back swaying in rhythm. The memory of sweat on that body after…after what? I was watching A★★★ dance from within a profound paralysis, an intense solitude, letting myself be invaded by every movement, feeling the tension of this immaterial thread that linked us even from a distance. Then a sudden invasion of anguish—looking at this body and knowing it to be ephemeral.

In the end what I loved above all else: those hips, narrow and broad at the same time, those legs that I never knew how to describe except, mundanely, as slim and long. But it wasn't this that made them desirable to me—when we made love, I couldn't stop caressing them, my lips against the inner thighs—it was something else, always something else, this indefinable something else where desire hides itself. Perhaps I was enticed by the slow motion of the dance, before my eyes, sublimely taking the body out of its rhythm.

Ephemeral, this body was undeniably ephemeral. I was overwhelmed by despair, vague and distant; I barely discerned the cause, buried as it must have been in ancient memory, abruptly rekindled and fighting to return, to take hold and actualize itself in a vision. Ephemeral—a word that I heard pronounced as a murder, as an image before my eyes, floating, tearing the veil; a living and funereal abrasion coming to break on the surface of anamnesis.

I had hoped that at least this hour of tragedy would provide me with a confidant, some faithful shadow attached to all that I was not able to bring into the light. What I had wanted to bury came back to me; there is no way to assassinate the cadaver I have been carrying in me for eternity, no way to dull the acidic decomposition that gnaws at me, torturing my flesh every time I find myself falling in love. I constructed each love too much in my own image. Did I want to collide against the jagged edges of suffering, to touch the infinitely collapsible floor of hell? And wasn't hell itself merely a pretext, in its essence ultimately denied?

"All the torments of romantic passion," I would say to myself sometimes, ironically. It was the repetition of the same torments that astonished me in particular. Seasons blended together: summer, autumn, winter, I never had any notion of time. My passion always seemed to be solitary or, rather, disconnected, unintelligible to myself or to others. Even Christ had not been alone; at least he had suffered in company, alongside two thieves. It was not that I had chosen solitude. In fact I suffered from it, but even the idea of passion seemed ridiculous and outdated, like something profoundly external, coming from an outside that was inaccessible to me, out of my reach.

Always failing, impaling myself on this fulcrum between speaking and keeping quiet, a knot was forming that I couldn't undo, little by little strangling my voice, cutting it off in a silence haunted by powerlessness. Rereading Stendhal and Flaubert at the time, their words, coursing through me, opened up a chasm in which my devastating powerlessness devoured me even more violently. Trying to forget through reading, I ended up forgetting everything, even reaching a state of self-oblivion, which alone is able to appease suffering: a blackout in the broken dream of this narrative. The only thing that managed to subsist in my eyes—lost and blind to everything else—was a dispossession that seized, embraced, and then released, without any more substance or intelligibility than that. It was an impossible task to set the boundaries of what I was, up to the edge where I blurred into the other—the indescribable other—so much did the meanings escape me, the words that others before me had uttered deep within an analogous attrition. I longed to reduce the impossible to the inessential, but I no longer had recourse to this principle of logic, which had suddenly become inadequate.

Inadequate, I would repeat the word to myself, my jaws clamping down on my breath, trying to choke it, to nip in the bud the inarticulate expressions that were surging and gnawing. Why give voice to the unarticulated? Because the inexpressible doesn't articulate itself in the least; it shatters into pieces before even taking form. I felt distinctly that something was breaking under a kind of assault; an obscure combat was taking place, syncopating my breath with its blows. At the impact of that secret confrontation, shuddering with a sadness only noticeable to myself, I pretended to be imperturbable.

Thus, forever oscillating between forced tranquility and irrepressible anguish, I was disconcerting those around me. And indeed, how was I to explain this apparent absurdity: that it is possible to have feelings, to suffer for them, and at the same time to be unable to cut oneself off from them or to have any contempt for them. These sentiments alone have wrested me from the inane inhumanity of my reclusive life spent between God, whom I wanted not to know, and an ennui that I could no longer break or abandon, as I had done too often by absorbing myself in unspeakable frivolities. These sentiments alone have been able to keep me from shamelessly abandoning myself to a life composed entirely of an empty and false legion of distractions.

What was I, truly? A drag queen of intellection, a gigolo of enamoration. A vile series of obscene appearances that had besieged my being without allowing it to escape the gradual stripping bare of its miserable suffering, despair obscurely making its way through my lonely soul. I was finally shedding my mask, my pride, through a fall and a superb defeat, a reduction to my most pure nothingness; such was my annihilation in those beloved arms.

I was swallowed up in the contemplation of this being, asleep, so close, seated and head drooping. I was looking at the bent neck, slender and dipped in shadow beneath a mass of hair. The slow rise and sure fall of breathing, the sudden jerks of consciousness that brusquely raise the oscillating head, which inevitably falls again, as if detached from the body.

I was struggling to discern in the shadows a bitter or desperate crease of the mouth. Arms crossed, folded in sleep over a resting heart, calm in its prison of ribs. That morning at the Apocryphe, while A★★★ was waiting for me to be able to leave the club, I was wondering what all the surroundings that besiege the sleeping senses—music, lights, voices—were becoming in A★★★'s dreams. What rhythmic effect was insinuating itself into A★★★'s sleep? I observed the circular and twitchy movement of the head, corrected in an effort of forced rigidity, straightened and then languid, surrendering to its own weight, straining the neck to the point of making me, watching, uneasy.

What did I get out of watching A★★★ sleep? I toyed with the desire to interrupt the fall of this head that, in an impulse of sudden tenderness, I could have encircled in my arms and pressed against my shoulder; I wanted to hold, to caress this face that a stray beam of light was illuminating miraculously, unveiling its bottom half as if it were detached, displayed separately from the rest of the body. A★★★'s legs were stretched over my knees. I didn't dare move, restraining the impulse of my muscles, normally so restless, I realized then. I was nothing but pure heat, pure momentary contact, a living support frozen in the observation of the other's shudders, those waves that move through the abandon of sleep. A★★★'s head was resting on its side so that the plane of the cheekbone was visible, skull slowly slipping against the mirror upon which it was leaning. Never before had this beloved body been so perfectly abandoned to my contemplation.

It felt as if I had never been permitted such transparency with anyone—anyone but A★★★. Had I confided more in A★★★ than in anybody else? What had I revealed? Had I unmasked myself, or at least what I thought I knew of myself? No, more likely I had exposed my own collapse, the ruin of the edifice I had so painfully constructed out of rhetoric and made to stand in for an identity. I was forcing myself to forget this nudity. My soul was not retreating behind a multitude of appearances that it could have incarnated endlessly, but rather, hollowed from the inside, was being instilled with doubt over this cavity that it hadn't filled with anything. I was then forced to recognize what I had always secretly wanted others to discover: "I" is nothing. It was a painful triumph when, faced with this beloved being, I finally achieved what I had always been aiming toward: the ability to confess my own weakness, my nothingness. But the weight of this nothingness was revealed only to me; it remained unintelligible to A★★★, and I remained in the barrenness, the ruin, at last revealed as if by accident, following this confrontation with my own nudity and death. "What am I," I was asking myself, "other than what you do not know how to say about me?"

Even when I was embracing this body, I suffered as if I had never held it in my arms, caught up in a love that was always uncompleting itself. Returning home one night, I found a T-shirt that belonged to A★★★ on the sofa in the living room left out from the night before; I searched in it for A★★★'s scent, for a trace that had not yet vanished. I closed my eyes and abandoned myself to a hopeless sweetness, head buried in the cloth as if it were a shroud, as if I were never to see A★★★ again. I constantly felt as though this body was lingering just out of reach, even when I was holding it in my arms. All I was ever embracing was the hopelessness of not being able to embrace; I was embracing an absence whose scent alone was penetrating me, breathed in from the folds of a T-shirt that had been forgotten and left on a sofa overnight.

I was blind, giving myself without a word, without a sign, existing as mere body heat. In my state of confusion I suddenly lost touch with reality. I was culpable, infinitely culpable for not having seen, for having been able not to see, for having sought a refuge that was too distant, inaccessible. Ever since, by achieving the coveted, powerful mastery of an indecent outward display of emotions, each more false and bitter than the next, I have fallen from betrayal into disgust, searching vainly for this love whose murder I never cease to expiate. What can I do, what can I give to escape from this morbid ennui, from the horrible clutches of this desire to embrace, from the stinging of tears I never managed to shed and from the hopelessness that seizes me so incessantly even while I seem to triumph. I travel; my work on the apophatic tradition has earned me some recognition within academia. They desire me, admire me, respect me...But of all those who will lament my death, how many will lament my life? The torture I endure from my inner thoughts plays out in a ridiculous drama—a tragedy of passion! How I love to mock myself. But I ridicule that which comes mortally to besiege me at those hours when I am unmasked, faced with my own abyss. I was remembering that face, the color of the air that winter day when we made love for the final time, not knowing that the bliss we were sharing then would be our last.

Since then, I have been able to discern only a carnal and obscene root at the core of all my relationships, which horrifies me. A★★★'s death caused me to unlearn sensual pleasure; I became caught up in carnal affairs, and I was tortured by the indignity of it all. Thenceforth, flesh became obscene to me. To clutch someone in my arms took on, without fail, a singular sense of indignity, the taste of putrefaction. When I embrace someone I am submerged in a feeling of infamy, in the nauseating sensation of having an orgasm in a charnel house, among the noxious fumes of decomposing flesh. I am revolted by flesh, but this revulsion, failing to deaden the assaults of my libido, merely infects them with a cadaverous terror.

I exist in a morbid state, my body riddled by consumption, not knowing from where to vomit up the soul it has created. For all I have done since A★★★'s death is forge myself a soul, and I no longer know if I should deny its existence. When I close my eyes, I see my soul as a screen crisscrossed with flowing, intertwined lines; architectural straight lines of a volume uncertain of its limits, exposed on all sides; a fragile construction, by turns knocked down, invaded, uprooted, robbed of its foundations, mined by all those embraces in which it happily prostitutes itself. Gazes, hands, all that is outside comes to burn it, shake it…But I would like to drown out the noise of this tearing of silk that happens between physical bodies and mental architecture. I am assailed by indifference. I had thought that I would never be able to grow tired of loving, but one night I woke to an absence of love and felt no torture: it was the absence of this torture that truly scared me, that tortured me.

I even regret the suffering that I felt. One morning at the Apocryphe, the night unraveling with no end in sight, I remember suffering from the feeling of being unfulfilled, from the incompleteness which was only continuing to grow between A★★★ and me. Noticing a sequin sparkling under A★★★'s eye, I imagined it was a tear, while I watched those lips murmuring the words of the Edith Piaf song that A★★★ had asked me to play so often: "La Ville Inconnue." My aptitude for suffering astonished me in that moment. I was suffering as no one suffers anymore in this century; my sensibility was outmoded in the extreme. Had I ever been capable of loving without suffering? And what was I suffering from, exactly? I would wait for nights on end, hoping that A★★★ would come and join me. I often despaired, staring at a watch that was engraving a revolting revelation on my living flesh. I would contort with pain on the rug; I loved more than I was loved, desired more than I was desired. My pride forbade me from admitting this suffering to A★★★. Or, more likely, my silence was the effect of a profound indifference. Perhaps I had only ever delighted in my own suffering, which I considered the purification of passions that, deep down, I judged as absurd.

Still dancing before my eyes are shooting stars, the dead embers of cigarettes, the firebrand of hasty breaths that interposed themselves between my hand and the surface of this body, tempting me like a demon, vanishing, encircling in its hand a pact signed with blood. Nothing but spilt blood between us, ever since the first day of our love; the day before, A★★★ had been cutting my hair and had inadvertently slashed the top of my ear with the scissors. I see A★★★'s face once more, ashamed and amused, in a hurry to grab cotton and alcohol to disinfect the cut that was bleeding onto my face. So much blood—it could only have finished in blood: this horrifying idea suddenly crossed my mind and I didn't know how to get rid of it. Blood continued to spurt, our love continued to pass through bloody fulgurations. Each time I could only say to myself with fright that it would finish in blood, whether mine or A★★★'s I hadn't decided. The violent, perhaps bloody, death of our love. I laughed one day thinking of my blood type: universal donor, O negative. I liked placing myself in universal negation, as a virus that had the power to spread in anyone without exception, a carrier of negativity. What a metaphor! It was thus that I was trying to escape from imagining this end that I wish I had never been capable of prophesying.

My memory tends toward its own eradication—my death—because I can no longer bear that I live, ever since that day when life appeared to me as a narrative, when I understood at last that by living this love, all I had been doing was enacting my cultural determinism. I had fulfilled the New Testament of this archaic, enormous Bible that had nourished my being. The Word was incarnating itself in death; the ancient prophecy was coming to fruition.

I suffered from not ever experiencing what is called "possession," and I doubtless owe this suffering to an enigmatic narrative that robbed me of myself. What I had wanted to possess, dead and inaccessible or perhaps even a purely abstract figure, condemned me to wander aimlessly from object of lust to object of love. Not asking them to be for me what I would have wanted to be for them, I lived in that most painful inequality of sentiments. I loved, but in full dispossession, haunted by betrayal.

I suffered from learning my nothingness, but, in trying to forget it, I took up and then successively abandoned all social simulacra. And I never suspected that the bottom of this hell was anywhere other than in myself, in an old biblical propensity for stories and for the infinite echo of the Word in search of its incarnations. I explain thus these waves of unintelligible and unfounded hopelessness, assailing me even while my mind was focused elsewhere, even as I was mechanically stringing together rehearsed gestures and thoughts. I was losing something of myself in an abyss of uncertainty. I was always attempting to take on a heavy burden of work in order to keep from being swallowed up by ennui, this first obsessive fear that nothing has ever managed to exorcise. Back then my strategy was to lose myself in order to find myself, which today I understand to be a mysticism; however, I had been deluding myself for so long that once I finally came to that realization, my life had already dissolved into waiting vainly for a death that was equally vain.

IV

Following A★★★'s death, I disavowed my job as DJ, just as my renown and reputation were beginning to grow. I was the object of ever more abundant solicitations which I evaded brutally. I was feeling the imperious need to break with all that had borne witness to the appearance and disappearance of the love I was mourning.

I handed in my resignation to George, who had no choice but to accept it. Initially I cloistered myself at home where I felt the painful lack of A★★★'s presence. I was trying to forget the void that had come to reside there, to escape from the proof of this absence through an unremitting stream of intellectual labor. But too often I would interrupt myself to think again and again about what I had lost. The thought pursued me, and my work was only able to hide me from it imperfectly; I was always slipping, the force keeping me from it was never sufficient. I would wander around the apartment aimlessly from room to room, recognizing here and there a trace, a sign, from the period of my life I had spent with A★★★.

Then I roamed, traveled for a few years, giving lectures in universities abroad to a select and very specialized audience. I was fleeing the incursions of my memory by constantly uprooting myself, always running, so much did I fear the moments when a prolonged hiatus let gather the points of reference I was trying to dissolve, when a spatial and temporal frame was able to reconstitute itself, bringing me back to the obsessive memory of this love. I was haunted by the possibility of settling into a place long enough for time's passing to become tangible.

I kept my apartment, which remained uninhabited except when I took brief trips back to Paris. I was living in part off of my intellectual activities, in part off of the fortune I had inherited from my grandmother. I became a strange sort of professor, attached three months to one university, spending the next six months as a visiting professor in another, going wherever I was welcome for a temporary title. In my suitcase I was always lugging around an essay I had been working on for three years, which an editor, in the city I was staying in at the time, had agreed to publish.

I had correspondents spread almost everywhere, and nowhere was I interested in having friends or lovers; my melancholy was rendering me more somber and taciturn than ever, and as a result I was repelling all sentiments other than esteem or indifference.

Returning to Paris after a week in Amsterdam, I found a letter from one of A★★★'s cousins, whom I had met during my first trip to New York. His letter, mailed a week earlier, was to inform me that A★★★'s mother was sick. Standing in the middle of my study, considering the letter I held between my fingers, I recalled that old woman whom I knew hardly at all. The thought of her distant solitude, lost in that cruel, cold city, choked me with remorse. I couldn't recollect her face, or anything else of her. Nothing. Except the surroundings: those streets, the avenues with the wind chasing around old newspapers; a nighttime vision of dilapidated facades in the deranged neon lights and lonely pedestrians swept along by the breeze. This city was a film noir before my eyes, mute in the silence of my apartment. I remained immobile for a long time, confronted with this unmoving vision.

In the morning, without having packed a suitcase, I took the first plane for New York. While my gaze was floating above the voluptuous mass of cumuli we had torn through while gaining altitude, I was haunted by the thought of this woman. I was thinking of her reclusive life surrounded by memories of the life that had abandoned her again and again. What I knew of her, what A★★★ had mentioned in passing in our conversations—seven years ago already—was coming back to me in fragments, little by little recomposing the details of her existence. There was a portrait of her as a young woman in a pink stole, painted after the war; I recalled her scandalous marriage with a bourgeois white man, the child (A★★★), the desertion and subsequent divorce that resulted in the child's fugues and eventual flight to Europe, only to return all too rarely. She kept the photographs of this devastated past in the drawer of a green, wooden writing desk. Did she ever look at them? I think she forced herself to forget, not to look, living between her bed, her somber work, and her kitchen where she made do with reheating the meals she no longer had the willpower to prepare for herself. When I knew her, already I perceived that she was exhausted with living, that she was carrying an intense lassitude inside of her, almost with arrogance.

A★★★'s death was the final blow. I imagined her scanning her room, looking down from the twelfth floor at the somber streets below, and beyond, at the elevated lights of the city; I imagined her eyes, no longer able to identify anything there that belonged to them. Closing my eyes, I could feel rising in me the tearless despair that had engulfed her, her child vanished and dead, her life dark and diminished with abandonment.

It took what felt like an infinite amount of time to get through customs at the airport; it was four in the afternoon when the taxi dropped me off at the hotel where, ever since my first trip to New York, I had resided for a few days until inquiring with some acquaintances about a place to stay. I took a shower. The city was cold and gray, almost murky. In the taxi on my way to the hospital, I peered out the window and tried to rediscover some of the formidable excitement that had filled my first visits: that taste of the bizarre, of the unknown and the variegated. My rhapsody ended in the blues. The hospital was a dreary composite of buildings of all sizes. For the length of three or four blocks, thrown pell-mell, was a conglomerate of successive additions hastily connected by footbridges or inexplicably juxtaposed and stacked: brick wall faces, domes, glass and steel towers, concrete cubes. A ramp, as one might find in an underground garage, brought visitors to the entrance. After a sort of decompression chamber formed by two successive doors, visitors passed from the frozen air of the exterior to a stifling and, to my nostrils, noxious atmosphere. Signs written in English and Spanish gave directions. In a stark hallway, I located an information desk and, introducing myself to the secretary, explained why I was there. She directed me to the intensive care unit.

The hospital was a labyrinth. I followed endless corridors, some cluttered with beds, and I crossed waiting rooms filled with miserable-looking people. I don't know what gave them such an appearance; not all of them seemed to be poor (I had only recently started learning to distinguish between misery and poverty). There were African Americans and Puerto Ricans seated, their elbows on their knees, staring at the ground between their feet; their winter clothes bothered them, they were hot and sweating, not daring to remove them. Their gaze would follow a nurse, a doctor, a guard, and then sink back into despondency.

I reached the unit that had been indicated to me and grabbed a nurse passing by in a hurry. She led me to the end of a transversal hallway: a bed had been wheeled against the wall, surrounded by a pole with an IV drip and a heart monitor. A canvas curtain, pulled around it imperfectly, was supposed to symbolically designate a space. The nurse warned me that the patient was weak but conscious. I approached. Her eyes were closed but she was not asleep. I saw on the heart monitor, displayed in a luminous trace, an excruciatingly irregular pulse; her belabored breathing was subject to brutal interruptions. I silently contemplated her face, now so thin, the white hair making a halo around this dark-skinned face, miraculously smooth and spared from wrinkles. Her left hand was resting on her chest; her right arm was immobilized by the IV, by the flow into her veins, drop by drop, of a colorless liquid.

When I put my hand on her forehead, she opened her eyes and stared at me, making an effort to recall a vague memory. I said to her very slowly, in an English so unsteady it made my voice tremble, that it was me, that I was here with her, that I hadn't forgotten her, that I was going to take care of her and that she was no longer alone.

She pronounced my name and caressed my hand, smiling. On the verge of tears, I clumsily gave her a kiss; she spoke in a murmur, asking me why I had been crazy enough to come all this way, saying that I shouldn't worry myself about her. She had straightened herself up to speak to me but was already drooping again onto her pillow, exhausted. Caressing her cheek, I told her not to talk, for I could see it was tiring her out. I took her hand in mine and, glancing at the heart monitor, saw with terror what it had cost her to speak: her heart was beating in a panicked rhythm that was taking a long time to subside. She nodded off, still clutching my hand. I lingered there, immobile at her side, repeating to myself, absurdly, "Ô mon Dieu, mon Dieu..." She awoke with a start, searching for me with eyes eaten away by anguish. They fixed on me and I felt her hand tense in mine. I leaned in and stammered derisory words of comfort in her ear. She said to me softly, almost inaudibly: "I've been waiting for so long for a voice like yours that could [a word I didn't understand] me." Her words, the tone of her voice, cut through me like a knife; I bit my lip.

I asked a nurse passing by about the possibility of procuring a quiet room for this woman, rather than a portion of the hallway exposed to incessant traffic. I committed myself to paying all the expenses that this regime might require. She went off to consult the head supervisor and returned soon after, accompanied by a nurse's aide who helped her to move the bed into a room twenty yards away. I took A***'s mother in my arms and placed her onto her new bed. She silently acquiesced. She was so still and light; it felt as if she had lost a lot of weight. I adjusted her nightshirt and put the sheet back over her body. She observed me as I took care of her, not saying a word; I could see nothing in her eyes except that she was following my every move.

The nurse replaced the IV bag; I went to see the doctor. He was in the hallway drinking a coffee. In clogs and a type of pajama that served as the uniform for the hospital health personnel, he seemed to be just as miserable as all the people I had passed in the labyrinth of hallways and waiting rooms. He was small; the harsh light coming from the ceiling gave him an unhealthy complexion and accentuated the faults in his skin. A troubling baldness hideously disfigured his scalp, lumpy and shiny with sweat; he frequently wiped his hand across his forehead. He volunteered the details of his diagnosis: long-term cardiovascular problems, blood pressure subject to brutal variations—she could fall into a coma at any moment. I gave him the contact information for my hotel, asking him to notify me if anything should happen, no matter the hour of the day or night.

When I returned to the room, the nurse had finished her tasks; as she was leaving, I slipped a twenty-dollar bill into her hand that she attempted to refuse. Once she had left, I approached the aged woman, her black skin contrasting with her white sheets. She asked me why I was doing all this for her. I searched for the words to respond: "It's a kind of debt toward A★★★...And you remind me of someone I would have wanted to be able to care for, as I now do for you...I have felt and I feel all that you've felt and feel. I'm almost a stranger to you but you're not to me..." She reached her hand toward my face; I knelt down by the bed and she wrapped her left arm around my head while caressing my hair. I could hear her heart beating and, as if in response, the discreet noise of the machine at every spike, a syncopated beep-beep in the silence of the room. I saw this dark-skinned hand and its pale, tidy nails out of the corner of my eye. With regret surging in me like a stifled sob, I thought of death, coming soon to consume all this.

Suddenly she said that I must be tired, that the trip must have worn me out. I swore to the contrary. She smiled and insisted that I return to my hotel to get some sleep, reassuring me that she was doing fine. It was night, what more could I do? My impotence took me by the heart. I promised to return the next morning at nine o'clock sharp, and kissed her on my way out. It was wrenching. In the hallway the nurse was approaching, carrying a tray of medications that she was about to distribute to the patients. I asked her to make sure to notify me at the slightest alarm. She asked me how I was connected to this woman, whom I was taking such good care of and with whom I seemed to share neither race, ancestry, nor even age. I didn't know how to respond and briefly explained that this woman was the mother of a person who had been very dear to me, who had died nearly seven years ago. She studied me; I don't know what was going through her mind. My features drooping with fatigue, my dark clothes, my foreign accent, this strange story, the color of my skin, death's repeated blow—what did she make of it all?

I went back through the hospital hallways in reverse. It was nine o'clock; the waiting rooms had been emptied. I passed nurses wheeling beds that had transported wailing women dressed in poor rags, cloth, and newspapers, or the silent injured. In a service elevator some people were attempting to pin onto a stretcher a black man howling and foaming at the mouth. Between two doors I caught sight of a woman waiting, terrorized and with an absent gaze, cradling a child in her arms. I remember that she was wearing a woolen bonnet and that she wore laddered stockings that fell over misshapen slippers. I walked the length of these hallways mechanically; the lights bathed the surfaces in a dirty yellow tint. In the big, deserted hall where I ended up at last, I saw security guards in uniform chatting and patrolling in pairs, walkie-talkies in their hands and revolvers in their belts. A sorrow bore into my ribs that I attributed to fatigue and to the effect of all the stimulants, coffee, and cigarettes I had consumed to ward off sleep. The footsteps of those around me dizzily diminished in my head.

The freezing night air hit me as I went up the ramp and gusts of wind whipped against my face; it had started to rain. On the avenue, cars were passing, inundating the building I had just left with light from their high beams. I was suddenly invaded with a dread of New York. Taxis passed me by, empty but not stopping. I started back toward my hotel on foot in the rain, twenty blocks of wet sidewalk reflecting the city and its lights in a blurred, murky image. I kept my head lowered, attempting to shield it from the brutal blasts of wind and the waves of rain. I saw New York only in a mirror of asphalt.

I walked straight up 42nd Street without noticing that I was rolling snippets of incoherent English around in my head: expressions and inter-jections that seemed to originate in songs I had heard long ago, when I was still with A★★★. I was searching for the lyrics to a particular song that we had enjoyed singing sometimes while walking at night through the streets of strange cities. Gradually the words came back to me, though I kept stumbling over the refrain:

> *Well hello then good old friend of mine.*
> *You've been reachin' for yourself for such a long time*
> *No need to explain, I'm not here to blame,*
> *I just wanna be the one to keep you from the rain*
> *From the rain.*
> *It's a long road when you're all alone*
> *And someone like you will always choose the long way home*
> *There's no right or wrong, I'm not here to blame*

I just wanna be the one (...)
And it's good to know my best friend has come home again
'cause I think of us like an old cliché
but it doesn't matter 'cause I love you anyway
Come in from the rain.

I tried to sing it to myself as I walked, but my voice cracked impossibly on the high notes. I took 42nd Street going west, walking with my head empty and my feet frozen. An old blues song came back to me, but I remained unable to sing; my soul probably wasn't yet sufficiently black.

Back in my room I ordered an herbal tea from room service. The television was emitting flashes of light, muffled echoes. From the window, high up, I was watching all that was down below: the intersections, the endless streets, the blanket of roofs punctured by skyscrapers and stained with lights blurred by the rain. I opened a window and the humid rumble of the city abruptly washed over my face. That odor of city rain, which, hot or cold, has always frozen my blood, surged forth like a spindrift of funereal nostalgia. I was snatched from it by the sound of the bellboy ringing at the door. He entered and placed the tray on a low table. I signed the bill, gave him a dollar tip, closed the door behind him and went back to my spot on the bed to drink my herbal tea. The TV screen and the screen of the glazed bay windows reflected the same insane scintillation. The tea filled me with a sweet warmth as I stretched out on the bed. My limbs felt shattered from all the distance they had traveled: the Atlantic, a hospital, and twenty blocks. Without even the strength to undress, I fell asleep feeling as though I were being crushed.

A sharp ringing woke me in the darkness of the dead of night. I groped for the telephone; the receptionist announced a name I didn't recognize.

It took me a few seconds to get a hold of myself, to accustom myself once more to the language, to realize where I was. I finally understood that I was being called from the hospital because the woman I was here to take care of had just suffered a serious drop in blood pressure—*blood pressure, blood pressure*, the phrase resonated in my brain as if on a loop, an interrupted feedback amplifying itself—had fallen into a coma, was going to die—*die, dying.* Yes, I had understood, I was on my way.

I hung up. I was cold—from lack of sleep, from the wet clothes I still had on, from the idea of this cold city. In the darkness, in my drowsiness, I sensed death in the air. I turned on the light and undressed; my gestures were slow, clumsy; it felt as if I were never going to be able to change into dry clothes. In the elevator I lit a cigarette, which made my head spin. In the mirror I was frightened by how pale I was. I thought I saw death on my face, in my eyes. How did that occur to me? There exists no image of death. I surprised myself, I suppose, by thinking, by knowing, or by understanding—I don't know which—that death lived inside of me, that death had come up to the surface in my sleep to take possession of my carnal covering, to put it on and to cover me in turn with its cast-off rag.

The night porter called me a taxi. I went down the same road I had taken a few hours earlier in reverse. I wasn't looking at the streets; I was trying to glimpse the reflection of my face in the glass that separated me from the driver, but it was too dirty and murky. My watch read ten o'clock, the time in Paris; I switched it to the time in New York. The sight of the hospital overwhelmed me. I lost myself in the hallways cluttered with beds. Cops were bringing in the hobos they had picked up in the street on stretchers; here and there were odors of sweat, vomit, urine, and disinfectant. The plastic double doors closed, swishing behind me. I hadn't run but I was out of breath. I sat for a moment between two chatting security guards before recommencing my haphazard route.

Was I dreaming? Deserted hallways followed cluttered corridors; it seemed as if I had crossed dozens of identical gazes, the empty stares of the New York night flotsam, and my own gaze was probably no different. A sign finally pointed me in the right direction. In a corridor identical to all the others, I spotted the night nurse in the middle of injecting a sedative into a woman who was babbling deliriously, pouring out an abstruse flood of Hispanic sounds. The young girl at her side was sobbing and wringing her hands, the tears hideously disfiguring her and revealing decayed incisors in her contorted mouth. When the nurse had finished, I approached her and she brought me to the room. The doctor was near the bed, speaking to the presiding nurse. They had placed an oxygen mask on the old woman's face. She had suffered a drop in blood pressure; as if there were nothing else to be done except wait for an unlikely miracle, the doctor withdrew. There was suddenly no one else in the room except for me and this body, whose breathing and failing heart depended on the machines. She didn't see me, probably didn't hear me either. With terror I drew my hand near hers, which remained inert. I leaned over her, observing her face. I spoke to her.

This dying woman was a painful reminder of her child. I pronounced the name of my beloved. An identical absence. And now, she was dying. Had she waited for me to come, for someone to come, before surrendering to her exhaustion with living? She had probably waited, with all her strength, for a voice to come and appease her long-lived solitude. What if she had died from despair, from the atrocious despair at having awaited a voice that never came? What if she had died in her bed, in this infernal hallway, always listening for the sound of a familiar footstep; amidst the noise, the deranged cries, the echoes of conversations, brushed by a thousand bodies, all foreign and indifferent. I kissed her forehead, wiped off the sweat, and thought about how on my dying day there probably wouldn't be anyone to do the same for me. I straightened up and lingered in silence, taking note of all the noises surrounding us, the beeps of the machines connected to her, the imperturbable rhythm of belabored breathing, the gaps of electronic silence…I went out into the hallway and asked the night guard for a coffee. I came back into the room and sat on the chair I had moved next to the bed. I held this old momma's dark-skinned hand in mine. I felt life beating savagely, shamefully within me; my heart resounded in its ribcage; my muscles, though spent by fatigue, played and moved in physical impatience. Life can be handed down, but not handed over, I thought to myself. The nurse entered and remained a moment in my company. I kept quiet while she talked to me about a number of things. She mentioned that her colleague had told her a bit about me. I told her my story, why I was there. I was speaking to her in a deep, hoarse voice without looking at her, caressing this hand I was clinging to lovingly. The nurse left soon after. I lingered in the penumbra, the only light coming from a lamp at the head of the bed. I was not at all aware of time's passing; my sole link to the world was the hand I was holding. I was looking at this face, searching for something of A★★★'s in it.

My rumination was interrupted by a sound. I turned my head but could not identify the source. Suddenly I understood that the noise was nothing but a sudden silence: the heart monitor had stopped beeping and a green, flat line passed continuously on the screen—the machine displayed a zero. I squeezed her hand in mine; I knew she was dead. Oxygen continued to flow, now useless. I called the nurse and the doctor. The doctor recorded the time of death, came back toward me and announced that it was all over. He asked me if I could take it upon myself to notify the family members, if there were any. And in the same tone, without transition, he asked me if I consented to an autopsy. Looking at the corpse, I was submerged in a kind of disgust at the abrupt resurgence of raw, cannibalistic reality. I responded without diverting my gaze that I judged autopsies to be barbaric and moreover of little scientific use, since they never yielded any new discoveries. I entreated him to excuse my refusal and thanked him for his care.

The nurse went about disconnecting all the machines hooked up to this body they had failed to keep alive. She explained to me what came next: declaration of death, retrieval of the deceased's personal effects from the hospital safe. I had to wait another two hours before the administrative services opened. I sat back down beside the cadaver. All my thoughts during those two hours of vigil were muddled and kept getting away from me; I felt nothing but an invasive inner turmoil, a mute silence without the succor of meditation. At eight o'clock I went down to the office to take care of the formalities. They gave me the clothes, the watch, and the bag that had belonged to the deceased. I inquired about a funeral home and they told me of one not far from the hospital. I went back into the room one last time. The waiting rooms were filling back up with patients. My body was cutting through the crowd, as if acting on its own; my soul seemed to be missing from it. The nurse on duty approached me to offer her condolences. I told her I would return the next day to settle the details of the burial.

The weight of it all, the heaviness and difficulty of the preparations, fell onto my shoulders. It had stopped raining, the sky had cleared, I saw the sun and upon leaving the hospital I felt the New York air, impalpable, enveloping me. I crossed the avenue, running, without seeing anything. I kept running all the way down the street to the building where the deceased had lived. It was a building with twenty floors, very close to the hospital. Closing the door of the studio behind me, I found myself again in the room that, since Paris, had been haunting me in a vision. It hadn't changed a bit, still a concretized shell of solitude where she had lived for years, neglecting her soul. I sat in the armchair, under her portrait done after the war. A★★★ had lived there too, before fleeing to Europe; in the closet were A★★★'s old schoolbooks and records. In a drawer of the desk against the wall I found a number of photographs and some letters A★★★ had written long ago. What was I supposed to do with all of this now?

I took care of all the practical details, notified the family, paid the priest and the undertaker. She was buried in a cemetery in north Harlem. Some of the family came to the funeral. I asked those whom I had met during my trips to New York with A★★★—the old mommas in tears, her sisters—to come by the apartment of the deceased to take anything they wanted to keep. Their sons regarded me strangely.

I had already made a packet of photographs, letters, and objects that I wanted to keep, which I assumed would not have interested the family because they held only sentimental value. I decided to stay another two weeks in New York and moved out of my hotel. The rent of the deceased's apartment, now empty, had been paid through the end of the month, so I started sleeping in a blanket on the floor.

I set about reading the letters from A★★★. I spread some photographs on the floor, and all day I tried to reconstitute those two lives affected so differently by a shared sundering. When I was hungry, I ordered Cantonese fried rice and sweet and sour chicken from the neighborhood Chinese restaurant. Every day, around five in the afternoon, I would go sit at a table in the Village to write down the story I had mentally reconstituted. I hadn't notified any of my New York acquaintances that I was in the city. At night I would go to a club without making the effort to meet or recognize anyone. People often did a double take when I passed, as if I had something written on my face, a declaration of my decomposition. One night, while I was waiting on the corner of 54th Street for a taxi, I saw a woman who also seemed to be waiting, staring at me.

She moved away from me swiftly, down the avenue. I was avoiding all company and in turn, for some obscure reason, people seemed to flee from me.

I left New York on a Thursday toward the end of December. America was absorbed in holiday festivities. It was cold; it snowed on the eve of my departure while I was walking toward Times Square. There was a great silence while the first snowflakes fell; handful by handful they prepared to bury the city, forming a shroud over the night that would soon turn to mud. I went back to the apartment and stretched out on the floor. I looked around me: it was night, the lights outside the windows and the lit but silent television projected onto the walls the shadows of the objects still remaining in the room. My back to the screen, I was observing the wall, alternately bluish and red. The shadows trembled and swayed with the rhythmic changes of lighting on the screen. Police car sirens and flashing lights passed rapidly along the avenue below. I was thinking about how this was the last time I would ever sleep in this apartment. This place, so strange, became estranged from me, and, above all, was lost. I was experiencing a premature nostalgia, which was sucking me into a state of melancholy; I was imagining all of this was closed off to me forever before I had even lost it. I saw people pass, rush before my eyes, and no one made me feel anything anymore. The world was dead and yet continued to strut upon its stage. In vain. Within three days, all of this would be dead to me, with no hope of remission. Walking in the streets, flying in planes, taking taxis had lost all meaning; there was no one waiting for me on the other side. This was the last place where something was still familiar. Henceforth everything would be exterior to me, the world a wasteland. I remained with eyes open, unable to escape the creeping sensation, insinuating itself in my flesh, that all was coming to an end. This old woman who had just died was, I suddenly realized, my last link to the world. There was no other. I no longer knew how to speak, those years of continued hopelessness had sealed my soul in a tomb, and nothing mattered to me anymore. All that had had meaning for me was now withdrawn—I hadn't been able to hold on to any of it—sucked back in like the sea, and I was turning into ice. Someone else would be living here soon; places and traces are swallowed up, disappear and erase themselves, wiping memory's slate clean. All these traces were disappearing and leaving me behind. I knew then that my destiny was only that: to linger on in a deserted world. I felt ice and injury, a fissure forevermore exposed to harsh blasts from the outside. I stayed quiet, unable to pay attention to anyone, absorbed entirely in my own horror, singular and inexpressible.

In the morning I went to the cemetery. Feet in the snow, I was standing before the tomb where the bodies of A*** and A***'s mother were resting. Their names were engraved on a black marble headstone. I wanted to pray but couldn't get past the first verse. The cold numbed my jaw and the words swirled within me; I couldn't pin them down. I wavered a bit, trembling with cold and despair, with powerlessness. I was thinking about this old woman whom I had barely had the time to know, lying beneath me and holding the white rose I had slid into her left hand just before the casket had been closed. And further down: my beloved, returned to dust.

I wanted to write down these two lives, these successive deaths that had annihilated my will to live, that had rendered senseless any project, any investment in a world to which I no longer had any ties. In fact it had become impossible for me to think of anything else; I needed to devote what was left of my willpower to undertaking the story of my beloved in the form of a biography, to be tidied up later once freed from the infinite reemergence of dispersed fragments in the wandering of waking dreams. Perhaps, if I were to accomplish this task, I would be delivered from the torture inflicted on me by the endless rumination and unruly resurgences that, rather than coming together to form a continuum, only thrust to the surface fractured and atrociously mutilated limbs. I settled into a modest hotel room in Amsterdam at the border of the red-light district and imposed a sort of house arrest upon myself.

This is where for two weeks in front of a typewriter I have endlessly forced my memory to purge itself of its possessor and, with the help of notes hastily made a long time ago or jotted down during my final days in New York, to retrace and reestablish the contours of this love.

V

I can finally type these words: THE END. My recollections are finally outlined and crystallized in imprinted phrases, no longer roaming incoherently through my memory. I am no longer living solely through remembering, trying to flee from the memory of these deaths I have at last put down in words.

I push back my chair, close the typewriter, and place it on the ground. Opposite me is a stack of pages, sitting atop the table that has served as my desk in this hotel room where I allocated my wandering. I crack the joints in my fingers one after another. I lean back and the chair cracks, too, under the pressure of my reclining. I stare at this miserable heap that has turned me into a recluse for the time it took to construct this narrative. I am powerless to free my gaze. What do I do now with this pile of paper, impossible to neatly classify as an essay, novel, or allegorical memoir?

At last, I wrest myself from this position. This hour is the last that I will have spent at the table that I forbade myself to leave before the thread of this ultimate unwinding of memory had been exhausted. And now I am, I think, free; I can rise and cross the threshold of the bedroom where I wove and imprisoned the vision transfixing me.

I can cast off my anchor and walk through the city streets, my mind delivered from the funereal brooding that kept leading me to the same abyss.

And so I rise, pushing the pile of pages to the upper left corner of the table. I unhook the jacket that upon my arrival I had relegated to the wardrobe, stinking of naphthalene. I stumble over the dinner tray I ordered earlier tonight (and every night for the past two weeks), turn the key, open the door and cross the threshold. The staircase is dark; it's eleven o'clock and tonight winter is spreading over the canals, turning them to ice. I walk aimlessly through streets, along quays, over bridges. I recognize a cabaret. Farther down, I pass a row of windows behind which women are exhibiting and offering themselves, to be consumed behind drawn curtains.

I plunge into the heart of this district given over to venality and artifice. The nearby port bordering the area sweeps the streets with a wind that brings odors of oil or sometimes of sewers. Brushed by this wind, skin takes on the taste of salt. I lean forward to escape from the onslaught of icy gusts that petrify the immobile bystander. The humidity permeates clothing and condenses above the canals in thick slabs of mist.

I lose myself in the silent and deserted areas, in the tranquil streets bordered by houses with darkened windows. Unintentionally, I deviate from my path and before me reappears the animation and furious illumination of this ghetto where people come to sell hell and flesh. A wide canal wraps around the cobblestone street where I push through a clotted mass of people. I cross over the canal, splashed with light, to its most distant border where the eddies slow; here it divides into three branches, forming a grid of diverging alleys. Conversations, which I had been catching in snippets as I walked by, stop resounding in my ears. On the other side of the canal, where I have just come from, I had swerved to avoid a screaming junkie who was rolling and contorting on the ground in the grips of withdrawal. From here, I see he is now being shooed away by two police officers attempting to grab hold of him.

The brisk wind strikes and assaults me with its breath as I step onto the path that runs the length of the canal. The farther I plunge, the more the alley darkens and narrows between the smooth black walls of successive warehouse facades and the abrupt edge of the quay where the tide breaks.

Two dark-skinned figures walk toward me, speaking loudly in a dialect that sounds like pidgin English. I hear the two men before being able to distinguish their features, and I keep walking without making eye contact. When I overtake them, they stop and approach me. They surround me in the cone of light diffused by a lone lamppost. The first lines of a poem I have been trying to recall for a few minutes reconstruct themselves in my mind. In a hollow of smashed pavement at my feet is a puddle of stagnant water frozen on the surface; it looks like a pane of ancient glass studded with detritus and trapped air bubbles.

The two men close in on me and speak to me brusquely; I see their eyes, bloodshot, fixed on me. I don't understand what they want from me. I tell them I have somewhere to be. I see the smaller, more nervous one pull a knife from his pocket and flit the blade, long, thin, sharp, before my eyes. My back to the canal, it's strange, I feel nothing…But I am haunted by these lines swirling through my head: "The virgin, lasting and lovely today/Will it crack for us with a drunken flap of the wing…"What were the next two lines, the crucial complement?

The deeper voice of the other man cuts through this dancing in my head. He is speaking rapidly; in his bursts of broken delivery I hear the word *money*, which is repeated by the little one in a voice rendered shrill with fear, haste, or excitement as he says, continually tearing at the air with his knife: "Giv'you'money!" I never have any cash on me; I am incapable of giving them what they want. But how can I prove it to them? I remain mute and immobile with the incompleteness of those lines continuing to plague me. It feels as if I have been standing, motionless, in this frozen décor for a very long time; I detach and distance myself from my body, now petrified. I gaze at it, upright at the edge of the canal, mirrored in the ice: the simulacrum and its reflection. My mind wanders, carried far away at the whim of those two lines in search of that symmetrical fragment which has disappeared into oblivion, the whole thus robbed of its meaning and harmony.

Suddenly, wrenching myself from my reverie, I shake my head and try to free myself, try to force a passage, to break the encirclement pushing me toward the edge of the canal. The man who had been standing unarmed at my left blocks me. I feel a blow to my back, an icy shard pierces my heart. Gripped with this frost, my chest contracts, all my attention rushing and contorting there. A vast silence; time's passage frozen, fixed, crystallized.

I feel my head hit a pane of glass, and yet—I didn't know I was falling. Sharp slivers jut out before my eyes, surrounding my skull with painful edges. The brush of a flap of a wing across my face, the caress of the feathers in the fan you were waving...Eden, Eden...

My body is wrested from the ground. My skull smashes through the pane of ice, which breaks into blades that slash my forehead and cheek, though I am unaware of it; a red veil hurtles down before my eyes, heat spreads through my skin. My body is no longer touching the ground; I feel it take flight, trying to balance, shunted about at the whim of the waves. A sudden muffled scalding at the bottom of my chest, the pain of a sundering wrests me from the mute dream that had been suspending the reality of the world around me. Suddenly I feel the inflicted pain; the suffering that I finally experience forces me to realize what is happening in this moment. The two men drag me to the edge of the quay and throw me into the void of a part of the canal that has not yet frozen over. In my death throes, as the waves of blood stream and escape from my back, I feel myself take flight. Then the split-second bedazzlement of a descending darkness into which I sink and lose myself.

In Anne Garréta's original French text, the narrator of *Sphinx* walks, overtakes, passes, is dragged along, is led places, follows, hurries, rushes, reaches, reaches on foot, sets foot, wanders, descends, ascends, climbs, strolls, promenades, returns, roams, roves, visits, meets people, joins people, travels, traverses, crosses, takes paths, gets lost, gets diverted, trundles along, flies away, and eventually sinks. Never does the narrator ever simply *go* anywhere. When I read the book for the first time, this never crossed my mind. It wasn't until I was translating the book that I asked myself why. The answer is, on the surface, relatively simple: to say "I went to the Apocryphe," the narrator would have to use the *passé composé* (the most common French tense used to describe actions already completed) and would have to say either "*je suis allé*" or "*je suis allée*." In other words, for the narrator to say that they simply *went* anywhere would require revealing his or her gender.

Sphinx is powerful because it refuses to do just that. At no point do we find out the gender of either the narrator or his or her love interest, and at no point does it matter to the story. Although written fourteen years before Garréta was asked in 2000 to join the experimental France-based literary group Oulipo (a portmanteau of *Ouvroir de littérature potentielle*, the Workshop for Potential Literature), *Sphinx* certainly follows in the footsteps of its members. Authors such as Georges Perec, Raymond Queneau, and Michelle Gringaud used linguistic constraint as a source of inspiration for their writing, for example in Perec's *La Disparition*, a lipogrammatic novel written entirely without the letter 'e.' Why did Garréta decide to write a genderless love story? Why this constraint? By omitting the supposedly ever-present phenomenon of gender, Garréta both reveals and undermines sex-based oppression, demonstrating that gender difference is not an important or necessary determinant of our amorous relationships or our identities but is rather something constructed purely in the realm of the social.

Taking inspiration from other authors working to overthrow the destructive construction of gender in Western society, such as Monique Wittig and Roland Barthes, Garréta set about subverting the way gender works in the French language in order to combat its sexist nature. French contains grammatical gender, meaning nouns are assigned either masculine or feminine gender, and pronouns and adjectives then take on agreement. On the other hand, English has semantic gender, meaning that inanimate objects are not assigned a gender, but people and living creatures are (with exceptions) referred to either as masculine or feminine. In French, the subject's gender can be identified as soon as there is agreement with a verb in the past tense or with an adjective, whereas in English the subject's gender can only be identified through personal pronouns and possessive adjectives.

Garréta believed that equality could not exist within a language that puts the two genders in opposition to each other, and so created a language and a world in which amorous relationships are not determined by a binary of distinction. This diffraction of constructed identities is an important aspect of queer theory, which Garréta defined at a talk in 2013 at Sciences Po in Paris as "an enterprise of deconstruction of categories that comprise a particular ontology of sexes and of sexualities." To read *Sphinx* is to engage in this deconstruction.

Translating *Sphinx* into English, I never had to deal with any of the verb tense agreement problems that Garréta was constantly confronted with. It would be impossible for a first-person narrator speaking in English to reveal his or her gender without speaking about it explicitly. And so the constraint of this Oulipian text at first seemed only to crop up in the sections in which the narrator speaks about A★★★, when I was faced with possessive adjectives at every turn. Garréta took advantage of the fact that, in French, gender agrees with the object, meaning that in the phrase *son bras, son* is in the masculine because *bras* is a masculine noun, not because the person the arm belongs to is a man, while in English this phrase would normally be translated as his or her arm. This rule of French grammar makes it difficult for those learning French to remember to refer to a thigh as "she" and a neck as "he," but provides a way for Garréta to avoid revealing the gender of her characters.

Where Garréta enlisted possessive adjectives to avoid gendered language, I alternated between four different strategies in English: using a demonstrative, dropping the article altogether, pluralizing, or repeating A★★★'s name. In other places, I rewrote certain passages to avoid personal pronouns, or applied adjectives directly to the subject rather than to something possessed by the subject. I broke Garréta's code by creating a new one. Because writing with a constraint does not add up to being constrained by your writing. Rather, it means bending your text to accommodate your ideas, interrogating the words of your language and finding out how they can be used to feed your whims.

But it would be missing the point to list the places where Garréta's text was one thing and mine became another. The constraint is in every sentence, every verb, every adjective of the French text. The entire narrative, almost every detail of the story and the style used to tell it, was shaped by the fact that there are no gender markers for the narrator or his or her lover, A★★★. The words wrap around their own limits, but without conforming to them; rather, the constraint and the writing become one and the same.

Focusing on the verbs in particular, the enormous difficulty of Garréta's enterprise becomes obvious, as does the masterful way Garréta made the text breathe within the framework she designed. In order to avoid gender agreement with certain verbs in the past tense, Garréta often uses the *imparfait* instead of the *passé composé*, but the imperfect tense implies an action that was repeated many times in the past or done regularly. And so the narrator, *je*, is always taking up habits: the habit of wandering, of skipping classes and studying for exams at home, of going to nightclubs with a priest, of playing the same songs while DJing, of visiting A★★★ before reporting for DJ duty, of sitting at a certain table at Café de Flore, of contemplating bodies, specifically A★★★'s body, of calling A★★★ on the phone every morning, of going into all kinds of bars and clubs and talking to mobsters and socialites alike, of staying up all night and sleeping during the day. Repetition can be boring, and the narrator knows it, constantly lamenting his or her state of ennui, his or her lack of a vocation and thus the endless aimless wandering, the mechanic repetition of mixing the turntables and talking to the same detestable people in the Apocryphe, the torturous cycles of fighting and making up with A★★★.

And actions that were not continuous? Garréta makes the *passé simple* work for her. The *passé simple* is the literary past tense, meaning a past tense used only in written French. It has no real equivalent in English, as it comes off as much higher in register and more unusual than our commonly used simple past tense (e.g. I went to the Apocryphe). Best of all, it does not require gender agreement, as do certain verbs in the *passé composé*. But it's not as simple as that. As I said, the *passé simple* is not commonly used. It sticks out. It wouldn't have been possible for Garréta to insert it wherever she needed to and then leave the rest of the verbs in the *passé composé*. In order to become natural, not to signal a linguistic constraint, it had to become a part of the text, but more than that, a part of the narrative. And so it becomes part of the narrator's identity—he or she is a rather pretentious, bourgeois(e) scholar who does not shy away from praising his or her own intelligence. One would expect for someone like *je* to use the *passé simple* in a memoir. And so even though in my *Sphinx* the narrator does not need to use a high literary style to avoid revealing his or her gender, this aspect of the narrator's personality is a part of Garréta's text that cannot simply disappear in translation.

In the same vein, although the English-speaking narrator might simply *go* places in my translation, my text has been inexorably infected by the strategies Garréta employed in hers. Lacking a good English equivalent to the *passé simple,* my text had to sway in a different way to craft the same personality for the narrator, accommodating elevated or unusual vocabulary when possible in order to keep the tone and register the same in English as in French. For example, by translating the French word *immondices* on page 45 of Garréta's text as "putrescence" instead of the more banal "filth" or "waste."

Similarly, Garréta often uses sentence fragments in order to avoid the verb altogether. Garréta turns this, too, into a part of the story, and the fragments enact what is being stated within the chopped clauses: *je* can only remember moments with A★★★ through fragments. Memory blurred, *je* can only describe bits and pieces of their time together, bits and pieces of A★★★'s body. And it doesn't stop there: the narrator is often in the company of men, whose gender takes precedence for agreement even if the narrator is a woman; *je* is often being dragged along places by other people, making *je* the object of the verb instead of the subject, requiring no gender agreement. None of the linguistic means Garréta employs to avoid using gender markers for the two lovers is obvious, nothing sticks out, everything is woven into the fabric of the narrative itself.

Including the language used to describe A★★★. The narrator can never describe A★★★ directly, as almost all adjectives in French have to agree with the gender of the person being described. Therefore, A★★★ is described indirectly. The narrator talks about A★★★'s skin, arms, shoulder, scent, residual imprint, thighs, mass of hair, curved neck, so that the adjectives agree with the gender of that particular body part in French and not with A★★★'s gender. A★★★ is also referred to as various nouns, including a spirit, a being, an other, a beautiful creature, a strange character, a phantomlike figure, a child, a vision, a funereal existence, a cadaver, a living cadaver, a life, a body, a beloved body, an inanimate body, an ephemeral body, a parasitic body, so that the adjectives agree with these nouns and, again, not with A★★★'s gender. Sometimes A★★★ is missing from the sentence altogether where there normally would be an object, for example when the narrator says, "*Je me surpris à desirer, douloureusement*" ("I was surprised to find myself desiring, painfully"), or "*Qu'était-ce? Regarder si longtemps dormir*" (literally: "What did I get out of watching [___] sleep?")—desiring who? Watching who sleep? Based on context, the object of these sentences is obvious, but there is still something missing—A★★★.

Because of the constraint Garréta chose for herself, A★★★'s character barely exists in the novel; A★★★ almost never speaks in his or her own words and doesn't seem to have a developed personality. The reader notices, and A★★★ notices too. Garréta doesn't gloss over this, but rather makes it the focal point of the novel. One night A★★★ reproaches *je* for dooming their relationship to failure from the start by engaging with only an image of A★★★, an image that did not correspond with reality, that forced *je* to mentally kill off the real A★★★ in order to enjoy a particular vision that alone was able to bring about *je*'s satisfaction. A devastating vampirization that happens in relationships no matter the genders of those involved.

Until now, there did not exist an English translation of a full-length work by a female Oulipian. And excluding this translation there does not yet exist a genderless love story written in English. Why not? And how can stepping into a universe where a relationship can be described without using gender markers expand our ways of thinking about love, desire, relationships? About gender? About identity? If our pre-conceived notions about all of these things are defied by this text, what does that say about our pre-conceived notions? Reading *Sphinx* is one way to think about these questions, to question our ways of thinking.

I owe an enormous thank you to Anne Garréta, Bernard Turle, and especially to Dan Gunn and the professors and students in the Masters of Cultural Translation at The American University of Paris for encouraging me to think and rethink these questions over the past year. My perceptions, my ideas, and my bookshelves are the better for it.

Emma Ramadan
Marrakech, 2015

ANNE GARRÉTA (born 1962) is the first member of the Oulipo to be born after its founding. A graduate of France's prestigious École normale supérieure, Garréta received her PhD from New York University in 1988. A lecturer at the University of Rennes II since 1995, Garréta has also taught at numerous American universities, and currently teaches at Duke University as a Research Professor of Literature and Romance Studies. Her first novel, *Sphinx* (Grasset, 1986), published when she was only twenty-three years old, was unanimously hailed by critics. Her second novel, *Ciels liquides* (Grasset, 1990), tells the fate of a character losing the use of language. In *La Décomposition* (Grasset, 1999), a serial killer methodically murders characters from Marcel Proust's *In Search of Lost Time*. She met Oulipian Jacques Roubaud in Vienna in 1993, and was invited to present her work at an Oulipo seminar in March 1994 and again in May 2000, which led to her invitation to join the Oulipo. She won France's prestigious Prix Médicis in 2002, awarded each year to an author whose "fame does not yet match their talent" (she is the second Oulipian to win the award—Georges Perec won in 1978), for her most recent novel, *Pas un jour* (Grasset, 2002), and she has served on the Prix Médicis judging committee since 2013.

EMMA RAMADAN is a graduate of Brown University, and received her Master's in Cultural Translation from the American University of Paris. Her translation of Anne Parian's *Monospace* will be published in the fall of 2015 by La Presse (Fence Books). She was awarded a 2014–2015 Fulbright grant for literary translation in Morocco.

DANIEL LEVIN BECKER is literary editor of *The Believer* and the youngest member of the Oulipo. His first book, *Many Subtle Channels: In Praise of Potential Literature*, was published by Harvard University Press in 2012.

Thank you all
for your support.
We do this
for you, and
could not do it
without you.

DEAR READERS,

Deep Vellum is a not-for-profit publishing house founded in 2013 with the threefold mission to publish international literature in English translation; to foster the art and craft of translation; and to build a more vibrant book culture in Dallas and beyond. We seek out works of literature that might otherwise never be published by larger publishing houses, works of lasting cultural value, and works that expand our understanding of what literature is and what it can do.

Operating as a nonprofit means that we rely on the generosity of donors, cultural organizations, and foundations to provide the basis of our operational budget. Deep Vellum has two donor levels, the LIGA DE ORO and the LIGA DEL SIGLO. Members at both levels provide generous donations that allow us to pursue an ambitious growth strategy to connect readers with the best works of literature and increase our understanding of the world. Members of the LIGA DE ORO and the LIGA DEL SIGLO receive customized benefits for their donations, including free books, invitations to special events, and named recognition in each book.

We also rely on subscriptions from readers like you to provide an invaluable ongoing investment in Deep Vellum that demonstrates a commitment to our editorial vision and mission. Subscribers are the bedrock of our support as we grow the readership for these amazing works of literature. The more subscribers we have, the more we can demonstrate to potential donors and bookstores alike the diverse support we receive and how we use it to grow our mission in ever-new, ever-innovative ways.

If you would like to get involved with Deep Vellum as a donor, subscriber, or volunteer, please contact us at deepvellum.org. We would love to hear from you.

Thank you all,

Will Evans, Publisher

LIGA DE ORO
($5,000+)
Anonymous (2)

LIGA DEL SIGLO
($1,000+)
Allred Capital Management

Ben Fountain

Judy Pollock

Loretta Siciliano

Lori Feathers

Mary Ann Thompson-Frenk & Joshua Frenk

Matthew Rittmayer

Meriwether Evans

Nick Storch

Stephen Bullock

DONORS

Alan Shockley	Cheryl Thompson	Meriwether Evans
Amrit Dhir	Christie Tull	Michael Reklis
Anonymous	Ed Nawotka	Mike Kaminsky
Andrew Yorke	Greg McConeghy	Mokhtar Ramadan
Bob & Katherine Penn	JJ Italiano	Nikki Gibson
Brandon Childress	Kay Cattarulla	Richard Meyer
Brandon Kennedy	Linda Nell Evans	Suejean Kim
Charles Dee Mitchell	Lissa Dunlay	Susan Carp
Charley Mitcherson	Maynard Thomson	Tim Perttula

SUBSCRIBERS

Adam Hetherington

Alan Shockley

Amanda Freitag

Angela Kennedy

Anonymous

Antonia Lloyd-Jones

Balthazar Simões

Barbara Graettinger

Ben Fountain

Ben Nichols

Betsy Morrison

Bill Fisher

Bjorn Beer

Bob & Mona Ball

Bradford Pearson

Brandon Kennedy

Brina Palencia

Charles Dee
   Mitchell

Cheryl Thompson

Chris Sweet

Christie Tull

Clint Harbour

Daniel Hahn

Darius Frasure

David Bristow

David Hopkins

David Lowery

David Shook

Dennis Humphries

Don & Donna Goertz

Ed Nawotka

Elizabeth Caplice

Erin Baker

Fiona Schlachter

Frank Merlino

George Henson

Gino Palencia

Grace Kenney

Greg McConeghy

Horatiu Matei

Jacob Siefring

Jacob Silverman

Jacobo Luna

James Crates

Jamie Richards

Jane Owen

Jane Watson

Jeanne Milazzo

Jeff Whittington

Jeremy Hughes

Joe Milazzo

Joel Garza

John Harvell

Joshua Edwin

Julia Pashin

Justin Childress

Kaleigh Emerson

Katherine McGuire

Kimberly Alexander

Krista Nightengale

Laura Tamayo

Lauren Shekari

Linda Nell Evans

Lissa Dunlay

Lytton Smith

Mac Tull

Marcia Lynx Qualey

Margaret Terwey

Mark Larson

Martha Gifford

Mary Ann Thompson-Frenk
   & Joshua Frenk

Matthew Rowe

Meaghan Corwin

Michael Holtmann

Mike Kaminsky

Naomi Firestone-Teeter

Neal Chuang

Nick Oxford

Nikki Gibson

Patrick Brown

Peter McCambridge

Shelby Vincent

Scot Roberts

Steven Norton

Susan B. Reese

Tess Lewis

Tim Kindseth

Todd Mostrog

Tom Bowden

Tony Fleo

Wendy Walker

Weston Monroe

Will Morrison